EXPOSING MAGIC

USA TODAY BESTSELLING AUTHOR
ALICIA RADES

Published by Crystallite Publishing.
Produced in the United States of America.
Cover design by Rebecca Frank.

To you.

"What are we going to do?"

"The only thing we can do, Cora. Prepare for what's coming."

Chancellor Harris's words echoed in my mind even after she left the hospital room. I lifted my head from my hands, and my gaze turned to Kellan's. He sat in the hospital bed looking as worried about Chancellor Harris's words as I was.

I'd screwed up. I screwed up big time. Our semester final had gone down in flames—literally. The only way to save Kellan from the burning building was to fly through the collapsed roof. The decision led to me exposing myself as supernatural, and the whole thing had gone viral. A stupid, stupid mistake—one I wouldn't take back for anything, because my partner was lying here beside me alive because of it.

"At least we get to go back to the academy," Kellan said.

I nodded, but my hands tightened around the armrests of the leather chair I sat in. Attending Harris Academy was all I ever wanted. I should have been relieved. And I was—on some level. But I couldn't get the rest of what Chancellor Harris had said out of my head. She seemed to think a war was coming, and she wanted Kellan and me safely within the walls of Harris Academy when that happened.

This world needs us, she'd said.

Hell yeah, they did. The Aedes and Davina had revolutionized the medical field. We *helped* people more than they could possibly imagine. Hell, it was because of us people healed so quickly and there were virtually no risks to surgery. And yet… people feared us.

People like Colt Walter, who'd threatened me the moment I exposed myself. For whatever reason, he hated us. I wouldn't let the rest of my people go down with me. I had to do whatever I could to fix this.

The sound of the door swinging open came from behind me. I turned to see a man in a black suit step into the room. He was tall, with short gray hair and age lines around his eyes. He looked like he could be a stock broker. I couldn't place my finger on it, but something about him chilled me to the bone.

Kellan sat up straight in the bed, fully alert. "Can we help you?"

The man cleared his throat and kept his eyes on Kellan. "I'm John Maddox, a Davina and Chief of the Public Relations department of the Alliance." Even his voice sounded terrifying. "I'm here to speak with Cora Marek."

My blood ran cold. Oh, shit. Was he here to arrest me or something?

I stood on shaky knees. "I'm Cora Marek."

Mister Maddox looked at me, but there wasn't an ounce of respect in his eyes. He folded his hands in front of him. "Miss Marek, I'm afraid you're going to have to come with me."

I froze. Kellan must've noticed my unease, because he reached out and took my hand. We both jumped at the contact. Kellan didn't like me like that. He was with Celina now. Still, his touch brought the nerves in my stomach to life. He squeezed my hand tightly, then pulled back, as if afraid to show any more affection toward me. We were, after all, only partners.

When my eyes met his, he gave me a firm look, as if to tell me I wasn't going anywhere with this guy.

I crossed my arms and turned back to Mister Maddox. "We can talk here. Whatever you have to say can be said in front of Kellan. He's my partner."

Maddox's lips tightened, like he was shocked a young girl like me had the balls to stand up to him. The truth was, I was quaking in my shoes, but I wasn't going to let it show.

"Very well," Maddox said stoically. He gestured for me to return to my seat, then moved across the room to stand at the foot of Kellan's bed.

I was relieved to sit back down again. I feared he was about to deliver some very bad news.

"As I'm sure you're well aware, Miss Marek, the events

of last night are not to be taken lightly." Maddox spoke in a slightly threatening tone. "What happened was… unfortunate."

The way he spoke didn't reflect his words. It was like he was choosing his words carefully as to not insult me to my face—like there were deliberate insults running behind his seemingly innocent words.

He continued. "The supernaturals have hidden their existence for ages. We must be diligent to keep it that way."

"Why?" I asked. The question slipped out before I could stop myself.

Maddox frowned, and his tone hardened. "To keep ourselves safe, of course."

I suddenly felt like I'd asked the stupidest question on the planet. I swallowed, but held my head high. "So, what's going to happen now?"

"Damage control," he answered bluntly.

"Wait, so she's not being prosecuted?" Kellan asked, looking relieved.

"The Alliance, of course, considered the possibility." The way Maddox spoke made it sound like he was on the side who wanted me prosecuted. I had the strangest urge to throw a ball of essence at his head. "But the board understands that this was an act of desperation. We don't believe Miss Marek poses a threat to exposing us in the future." He sounded doubtful, like if it were up to him, I'd be rotting in a supernatural prison by now. "Even if she did, prosecuting Miss Marek would look bad…"

Maddox trailed off. He'd said too much. It was obvious what he was about to say. My parents were so high-profile that this sort of thing would make national news within the supernatural community. Too many Aedes and Davina would take my side, and it would damage the Alliance's image. Thank God for famous parents, right?

Maddox cleared his throat. "The Alliance is willing to offer you a deal, Miss Marek."

My mouth went dry. "What kind of deal?"

Maddox paused a moment, as if deliberately dragging out the suspense. "We want you to go public and tell the world the entire thing was a hoax."

"What?" I balked. "How am I supposed to convince them of that?"

Maddox eyed me up and down with a look of disgust. "That's for you to figure out."

What the hell was this guy's problem? I'd never met him before, and already he hated me.

I lifted my chin. "And what happens if I don't take the deal?"

Maddox smirked, like he'd like to see me try. "Exposing the Aedes and Davina in a criminal offense, Miss Marek. You're lucky the Alliance is forgiving this incident as an accident and giving you a chance to fix it."

Kellan's eyes darkened, and his tone became harsh as he repeated my question. "What happens if she doesn't take the deal?"

"What happens to all criminals, Mister Greene?" Maddox practically sang, as if calling me a criminal pleased him. "She'll be imprisoned for her crimes."

My stomach plummeted to my toes. No way in hell. I

wasn't some sort of traitor. I did what I had to do to save Kellan's life.

And now I had to do everything to save mine.

I crossed my arms and got to my feet. "Fine. I'll do it. I'll convince them."

"No, Miss Marek." Maddox chuckled, and it sent a shiver down my spine. "Convince *me*."

2

My heart pummeled against my rib cage as Maddox left the room. The white walls spun around me as I lowered myself back into the chair. Convince John Maddox? How was I supposed to do that?

"Cora. Cora." Kellan's voice sounded like it was coming through a thick vat of jelly. I barely heard him.

Once the initial shock waned, I lifted my head to meet Kellan's gaze. "What am I supposed to do? If I can't convince him, I could end up—"

"Relax, Cora," Kellan said in a soothing tone. It was weird to hear him reassure me like that. Normally, we were yelling insults at each other. "We'll figure something out."

I furrowed my brow. "Like what?"

Kellan smirked. "I have an idea."

〰

"Are you sure this is going to work?" I asked.

Our friends had already come and gone, and Kellan and I were alone. We'd been rehearsing for an hour already. He had a great idea. The only problem was I didn't know how well I could pull it off.

"For sure," he said confidently.

Kellan pushed the bed sheets off his legs and stood on shaky knees. The wound on his leg had been healed, but he'd lost a lot of blood and hadn't eaten much since last night. Until this morning, he'd been hooked up to tubes to help with the dehydration.

My gaze roamed up and down his body. I didn't mean to check him out; I was just concerned about him. But looking at him made my cheeks flame nonetheless. "Are you sure you're up for this right now?"

Kellan placed a hand on my shoulder. "Absolutely. We've got this, partner."

Butterflies danced in my stomach when he called me his partner. It was stupid, because we'd been paired up all semester, but something about hearing that word come from his mouth made it seem… sexy.

I raised an eyebrow as I looked over his hospital gown. "Are you wearing that?"

Kellan chuckled. "No. Celina brought me clothes this morning. I'm going to change."

The mention of Celina made my guts sink. What did he see in her anyway?

Kellan reached for the curtain beside his bed but paused before tugging on it. He winked at me. "No peeking."

"Please," I scoffed. "Like I want to see *that*."

I did. I *so* did. But no way in hell was I going to tell him that.

Kellan rolled his eyes, then pulled the curtain between us and began getting dressed. "All you have to do is be confident," Kellan said from behind the curtain. "Believe it yourself."

"How can I believe in something I know is a lie?" I asked.

"You just… pretend, I guess," he said.

"Pretending is the exact opposite of believing," I pointed out.

Kellan whipped the curtain back, and I jumped a little. I went still the moment my eyes fell upon his torso. He wore jeans that hung off his hips in a way that made me want to drool, and his black shirt lay tight across his muscled chest. The color reminded me of his wings, which made me hot just thinking about. He was hella sexy when he went shirtless and took his feathery black wings out.

Crap. How was I going to focus at all this semester now that I knew I had feelings for my partner?

I shook the thought off. I didn't need to be thinking about any of that right now.

"Let's practice," Kellan said. He sat on the bed again and looked me in the eyes.

Damn it. Taking him off my mind was *not* going to work when he looked at me with that smoldering gaze.

"I'm going to ask you a series of questions," he said. "And I want you to make me believe the lie."

I shifted in my chair. "Okay…"

"What's your name?"

I hesitated. Nothing but my real name came to mind.

"Err." Kellan mimicked the sound of a buzzer. "You hesitated too long. Now I'm not going to believe anything you say. Let's go again. What's your name?"

"Shay—Laura," I answered, stumbling over my words. My two friends' names got mixed up in my mind.

Kellan raised an eyebrow. "Shaylaura?"

I bit my lower lip. "No?"

I mentally kicked myself. Why was I being all shy and weird around him? I wasn't normally like this. Damn hormones.

Kellan sighed. "Rule number one about lying, go with your first instinct. Rule number two, never change your mind. Rule number three, always answer with yes."

"Oh, so you're an expert at lying now?" I teased.

He chuckled lightly. "You'd be surprised."

"Hang on." I crossed my arms. "What exactly have you been lying about?"

"Nothing," he assured me.

"See, now how do I know *that's* not a lie?" I pointed out.

His tone softened. "Because I don't lie to you, Cora."

My heart lifted in my chest. I didn't care how good of a liar Kellan was. When he said those words, I believed him wholeheartedly.

Kellan clapped his hands. "Again. What's your name?"

The first name that popped into my head was my mother's, so I went with it. "Kathryn Marek."

"Where did you grow up?" he asked.

Eagle Valley came to mind, but I was supposed to lie, so

I went with the next thing I could come up with. "Right here in Celia, Minnesota."

He started throwing questions at me faster and faster. "What's your favorite pizza topping?"

"Mushrooms," I lied. Pepperoni all the way.

"Favorite hobby?"

"Ice skating." If I sounded convincing, it was a miracle. I'd actually never been ice skating before. My favorite hobby was collecting antiques.

"What's your element?"

"Fi—water."

Kellan frowned, but he continued anyway. "What's your major?"

"Surgical studies," I spat out before I could question it.

"Which are you: A morning person or a night owl?"

"Night owl."

"Do you love me?"

"Yes." The word slipped out before I could stop myself. My entire body went rigid, and I held my breath as I awaited his reaction. I hadn't even known until that moment that I felt that deeply about him. Of course I knew I was crushing on him, but *love*? Deep down in my soul, I felt the truth to my answer. I loved Kellan Greene.

A smile spread across Kellan's face. Time seemed to stand still, and my mind raced with theories to what it meant. Was he going to say it back?

"See?" Kellan said. "You're already a pro at this."

I released the breath I was holding, but with it came the sinking of my stomach. Of course Kellan thought I was lying. It was part of the game.

"Are you ready?" he asked.

"As I'll ever be," I answered, trying to keep my tone steady. "Let's get this over with."

"Let's do it over here." Kellan pointed to an empty corner of the room. "It's not quite as convincing when people can tell we're in a hospital room, is it?"

"No, it's not."

Kellan and I pulled two chairs together, and I took out my phone. My hands shook a little. If I didn't get this right, that jerk from the Alliance was going to make sure I was put on trial for exposing us. It was a lot of pressure to put on a girl.

Kellan nudged me in the side, making me nervous for entirely different reasons. "Nervous?"

"Of course not," I lied. "I don't get nervous."

"Good job," he praised. "Even *I* believed that one."

I rolled my eyes at him.

"Okay, let's go," he said.

I pulled up my camera app and paused. I shoved my phone in his direction. "You do it."

He pushed the phone back. "That Public Relations guy wanted you to do it."

"Ugh," I groaned. "At least help me out, okay?"

Kellan nodded. "Of course, partner."

I mentally swatted away the butterflies in my stomach and swallowed my nerves, then pressed *record*.

"Hello, Internet!" I practically sang. Oh, God. I didn't sound *anything* like myself. It was sickening. "I'm Cora Marek."

"And I'm Kellan Greene," he cut in like we'd practiced.

"And we have a confession to make," I said.

I didn't like using my real name, but Kellan thought it was best to put some truth into the lie. It would make the rest of it more believable when people started digging for confirmation.

"You don't know who we are, but by now you've *seen* us," I continued. "Last night, we performed an experiment for our social media class. There are no words for how incredible this experience has been."

"We're definitely getting an A," Kellan joked.

"For sure," I played along. "By now, you've all seen the video of what *looks* like an angel flying out of a burning building to save an injured man. Well, we hate to burst your bubble, but it was all fake." I put on my best expression of disappointment.

Kellan subbed in for me. "See, while our classmates were testing for their final in firefighting, Cora and I were preparing *our* final for our social media class. The assignment was to create something that would get the highest number of likes, shares, clicks, you name it. Of course, we thought the best way to do that was to put on a show."

Kellan was such a natural at this. If I didn't know what had really happened, I'd have believed every word he said.

"With the help of our professors, we got in costume, hooked up to some wires, and made it look like an angel was flying out of the flames," Kellan said.

"Well, I mean, it was a little more complicated than that," I joked. "But we won't go into all the specifics. We just wanted to let everyone know that the videos aren't real. We really would've loved to see how much farther this could go, but we already have plenty of data for our class, so we thought it was best to tell everyone the truth."

Crap. I was rambling now. Time to wrap it up.

"If you guys see a real angel, let us know," Kellan laughed. "But for now, it's just the brainchild of two college kids who wanted to see how far they could go on social media. Again, thank you guys for all the likes and shares. If you want to stay updated, we've got links in the description, and don't forget to hit that follow button before you leave. *Chao!*"

I held my smile until I hit the button to stop recording. I turned to Kellan with both my eyebrows raised.

"What?" he asked innocently.

"You're a natural," I complimented.

He scoffed and rolled his eyes.

"No, I really mean it," I said.

Kellan shrugged. "It's nothing. I used to run my own channel."

My jaw dropped. "I didn't know that. What was your username?"

I turned to my phone and scrolled through the apps.

Kellan groaned. "Oh, come on. Don't go looking for it. It's so cringe-worthy. There's a reason I stopped."

"I want to check it out," I insisted.

Kellan leaned over to grab my phone out of my hand, but I held it out of reach. Good God. He was almost on top of me now. "Cora," he complained.

I laughed. "It can't be that bad."

"Oh yeah?" he challenged. "Maybe we should go look at your photos and videos from five years ago?"

My laughter instantly died, and the blood drained from my face. "How about no?"

"See?" he said.

I let it drop, while secretly making a mental note to search his channel later. "How was our first take?" I asked. "Do you think it was good enough?"

"I think it was perfect," he told me. "The first one is always the most natural."

I snorted. "Says you."

"I did say so," he teased. "Are you ready to tell the world the truth?"

I rolled my eyes. "You mean the lie?"

He narrowed his eyes. "But is it?"

"Yes," I deadpanned.

Kellan frowned. "Cora, if you're going to stick to this lie, you've got to believe in it yourself. So let me ask you again. Are you ready to tell the world the truth?"

I straightened my spine and saluted him. "Yes, sir."

Kellan chuckled and shook his head. "You're such a nerd."

"Hey! I wear the title of *nerd* proudly, thank you very much."

Kellan got serious. "Cora, you're stalling."

My shoulders fell. "Okay, maybe I am."

"Send me the video, and we'll do this together," Kellan offered.

"Okay," I agreed. "Together."

3

$\mathcal{I}$ held my breath as Kellan and I blasted the video across social media. I couldn't take my eyes off my phone, waiting for the numbers to start climbing. My stomach sank as it became more and more apparent that this video wasn't going to go viral as quickly as the last.

And then something miraculous happened. All at once, it seemed like comments started flooding in to Kellan's account. He already had a huge following, so when his followers started sharing it, it was like we couldn't turn off the flood of comments.

Of course Kellan would do something like this. It's so like him.

Congrats on pulling it off, buddy!

I knew it! I kept telling people the video was faked.

I looked back at the original, and you can totally see the wires holding them up.

I breathed a sigh of relief.

"See?" Kellan asked brightly. "I told you everything would all work out."

I frowned as my eyes scanned a new comment. "Apparently, not everyone believes us."

Angels are real! This video is the real hoax!

And then came a long rant from another commenter who called us sick for using someone's religion in our social experiment. *I hope you eat a ghost pepper and choke on it!*

"Forget about them," Kellan said. "They're just trolls."

"What about the people who don't believe us?" I asked.

"We don't need everyone to believe us," Kellan reminded me. "Just enough to mark those videos as unreliable."

"True," I sighed, standing from my chair. "I think I need a break from all these comments. I'm going to head to the cafeteria and bring you back something to eat."

"You don't have to do that, Cora," he assured me. He didn't sound like he was just being kind, either. He sounded like he meant it.

"You don't really have a choice," I told him. "You're still recovering from the blood loss, and you need something to keep your strength up. Until they discharge you, I'm here to take care of you."

Kellan leaned back in his bed and made a show of snuggling in. "In that case, bring me back chocolate."

"Okay, your Highness."

Kellan grinned as I headed out the door.

The hospital was quiet as I started down the hall. I finally had a chance to breathe, and everything that had happened over the last twenty-four hours began racing through my mind—the test, how Celina had sabotaged it, and Kellan showed up to help, how the roof had caved in and I had to fly Kellan out... Colt's threat to me, Chancellor Harris's visit, everything John Maddox had said. It was all so much to absorb. I didn't even know where to start with it all.

My mind wandered so far that I didn't realize where I was going. I missed the turn to the cafeteria and started weaving through the maze of hallways. I didn't realize where I'd ended up until I heard the sound of a voice coming from one of the open doorways.

"Hey! It's her! Hey, lady!"

I backpedaled a few steps and looked into the room to see two girls lying on identical beds. The older of the two must've been at least ten years old, but she was barely alert. She was attached to a bunch of tubes, and her lips were pale. Whatever happened to her must've been really serious if the Davina hadn't healed her yet.

The other girl looked around six, and she was very cheerful as she poked at a tablet in her lap. My gaze darted up and down the hall, and I wondered if they were alone. I didn't see anyone nearby who could be their parents.

"It's you!" The younger child smiled brightly at me and held up her tablet. The video from last night played on the screen. "You're the angel. Are you here for Rebecca?"

My face paled, and I stepped closer to the room. Kellan's words echoed in my mind. I had to stick to this lie and believe it myself.

I shook my head. "I'm sorry, but I'm not an angel."

"You look like one," she told me.

My heart melted on the spot. The way she looked up at me with those big brown eyes made me want to cry.

"Thank you," I said. "You and your sister look like angels, too. You are sisters, right?"

They shared the same curls and chocolate eyes.

The young girl nodded. "I'm Saddie, and that's my sister Rebecca."

"It's Becca, Little Mouse," her sister corrected her. She spoke in a strained voice, which only tugged on my heartstrings further. I still couldn't figure out why she'd been hooked up to all those tubes, not when there were Davina healers on staff.

"What are you two doing here?" I asked curiously. "Where are your parents?"

Saddie frowned and spoke in a serious tone. "Grandpa doesn't like it when we talk about them."

My stomach sank. "I'm sorry. Is your grandpa around?"

"No," Saddie said. "He had to leave to get cigarettes."

"Saddie," Becca hissed, but she didn't stop talking.

"We were in a car accident," Saddie announced. "But I'm all healed up. See?"

Saddie held out her arm and pointed to nothing. She must've had a nasty gash or broken bone the way she looked at it so proudly, but the Davina had already healed her.

"Not me, though." Becca's gaze fell.

"What's wrong?" My voice filled with concern.

"It's normal for her," Saddie told me matter-of-factly. "She's *always* in the hospital."

"Not *always*," Becca shot back, before looking to me. "My immune system doesn't work right. I don't heal as fast as Saddie."

My heart fell. On the outside, Becca looked okay. There were no lacerations or bruises that I could see. But I'd learned in my classes that chronic, wide-spread conditions were difficult to heal with essence. We had to be able to pinpoint the site of the injury and direct our magic into it with care, or we risked hurting our patients even more. It was why we could heal cancerous tumors easily but not wide-spread cancers like those in the blood. It was the same with chronic conditions like immune deficiencies. We could help speed the healing process along, but if the body wasn't working right to begin with, our essence could only help so much. The body had to do the rest of the work itself.

Saddie studied her tablet closer. "Do *you* have a sister?"

"No, I—"

I cut off as she turned the tablet screen back toward me. It was the same video from last night, when I flew out of the burning building, but this time it was zoomed in on my face so I was easily recognizable.

"She looks just like you," Saddie accused.

Rebecca's gaze darted to the screen, then she narrowed her eyes at me. "Why are you lying to us?"

"Lying?" I balked.

"You said you're not an angel, but that's you." Rebecca pointed to the tablet.

"It is," I admitted, "but—"

Tears welled in Rebecca's eyes. She bit her lower lip,

and it nearly tore my heart to shreds. I couldn't stand to see *children* like this. I was a Davina. I should be able to heal them.

"Have you come to take me to heaven?" Rebecca asked as a single tear fell down her cheek.

"No, of course not." Instinct took over, and I rushed to her bedside. I knelt beside her and ran my thumb along her cheek to wipe away the tear.

I opened my mouth and waited for the lie to come, to tell the girls the video was nothing more than a trick. But a hollowness opened in my stomach, swallowing the words.

Rebecca spoke before I could. "Tell me the truth. What's going to happen when I die?"

Rebecca's eyes gleamed as she looked up to me, and my guts sank. In that moment, something inside of me changed.

I was suddenly taken back to the time when my best friend Kaylee fell out of our treehouse and broke her arm when we were nine. Kaylee was tough and refused to let anyone see her cry—until we were alone in the hospital. She turned to me and said, *"Promise me I'm not going to die, Cora."*

Rebecca gave me that same pleading expression. I knew in that moment I couldn't lie to her. Rebecca was just ten years old, and already she'd been worn down by her pain. The least I could do was offer her comfort—to serve and heal. That was what it meant to be a Davina.

I took a deep breath and reached out for her hand. "When you die, your essence will be restored to the earth."

Rebecca blinked away the tears. "Essence?"

"Your soul energy," I clarified. "You'll be reunited with all the people who died before you. And you'll become a part of everyone who comes after you. You'll feel nothing but peace. It's a wonderful, beautiful process."

Crap. Now *my* eyes were watering.

Rebecca's eyes cleared, and a smile tugged at the corners of her lips. "So I'm going to be okay?"

I nodded. "Of course you are. But it's not your time yet, Becca."

I couldn't know that for sure, but it felt like the right thing to say.

"What do I do?" she asked. "What do I do before my time is up?"

I squeezed her hand. I didn't know what to say, but the words started tumbling out of me before I knew what I was saying. "You find your purpose, Becca."

"What's my purpose?" she questioned.

"It's whatever you want it to be," I told her. "You get to decide what you want your legacy to be, Becca. The world is a scary place, but each and every one of us get to add our own beauty to it."

Becca closed her eyes, and her lips stretched into a wide smile as she relaxed into the pillow. "I like pretty things."

"Like unicorns," Saddie cut in.

Becca chuckled. "Yeah, Little Mouse. And wings." Becca opened her eyes again and looked at me. "Can you show me yours?"

Every muscle in my body tensed. I glanced toward the door, but Saddie had already jumped out of bed and was closing the curtain on the other side of the bed.

"Yes, show us!" Saddie sang as she jumped back onto her bed.

I hesitated. "I- I can't. Not here."

Becca's bottom lip poked into a pout, and Saddie frowned.

"Please?" Saddie begged.

"We won't tell anyone," Becca promised. "We swear it."

I couldn't. Exposing myself was a huge offense. I already had one strike against me. The Alliance would never forgive me if they found out about this.

If...

I stopped and seriously contemplated what to do. These girls looked at me like they needed hope in their lives. If I wanted to leave anything behind when *I* died, it was inspiring others to do good. For as long as I could remember, all I wanted was to make the world a better place—to make a difference. In that moment, a sense of peace washed over me when I realized I had the opportunity to do just that in these two little girls' lives.

"Okay," I agreed.

The girls' eyes lit up in unison.

My heart pounded. I couldn't believe what I'd just said. I'd just agreed to break the law, to go against the Alliance *again*. And the weird thing was, *I didn't care*.

I took a deep breath and stood, then flexed my shoulders. Glorious white feathered wings grew from my back as I shifted into my Davina form. They fit perfectly past the straps of my tank top. The two girls drew a breath in unison, and their eyes widened.

"So beautiful..." Saddie whispered.

Her sister had gone speechless. She threw her hand over her mouth, and the tears returned to her eyes. But they were no longer tears of sadness. They were tears of joy, and that filled my heart to the very brim, until it felt as if my emotions were overflowing.

"You've made me so happy," Becca whispered.

In that moment, I knew I made the right choice by showing them my wings.

4

I couldn't stop thinking about Saddie and Becca, even after I left the hospital. I didn't tell Kellan about what I'd done. I knew he would only chastise me for it.

Luckily, we didn't talk much over the next week, so even if I wanted to break down and confess, I couldn't. It was winter break, and I was staying at my parents' while Kellan went back to Iowa to visit his family for Christmas. I should've been spending time with my parents, but I spent most of my time in my room, going over everything that had happened.

I wished I could see those girls again. I had to know—did exposing myself leave a lasting impact on them?

Of course it did. They were ten and six. That was the kind of thing you remembered your whole life.

Oh, crap. Did I make a mistake? They were just children now, but of *course* they would grow up someday. Would

25

exposing myself come back to hurt my people in the future?

I jumped out of bed when the thought hit, and I scrambled over to my laptop across the room. I pulled it onto my lap as I snuggled back under the covers. I furiously typed into the search bar and brought up endless stories of people who claimed to have near-death experiences and interactions with angels. I sat there for hours listening to video interviews and reading first-hand accounts. I didn't know what I was looking for, but I couldn't keep from diving deeper into the stories.

Hours later, the doorbell rang. I didn't think anything of it until I heard my mom's voice calling me from downstairs.

"Cora!"

I paused the video I was watching and set my laptop aside. I was still in my pajamas, and I wore Kellan's sweatshirt I still hadn't returned to him. My hair was tied into a high ponytail, and I wasn't wearing any makeup. I furrowed my brow as I got out of bed, wondering who could possibly be here. I headed over to the window, and my heart stalled in my chest when I saw the vehicle parked in the driveway.

"Oh my God!" I cried. I raced across the room and flung the door open, then tore down the hall and pounded down the stairs.

"Kaylee!" I screamed as I ran into the living room.

My best friend from high school stood just inside the door. She wore a huge smile and spread her arms out wide.

I slammed into her, pulling her into a tight hug. She squeezed me back and lifted me off the ground.

"Cora! I missed you so much!" she cried.

She set me down, and I stepped back to look her up and down. Kaylee looked the same as always. She was several inches taller than me, with long flowing brown hair and beautiful eyes. But there was something different about her, too. There was a glow to her that I'd never noticed before. Her brunette hair seemed more vibrant, and a touch of a smile lit up her face.

"I can't believe you're back from Europe," I said. "I thought you had at least six months left."

"Oh, I do," she replied in an excited tone. "I came back for Christmas. After New Year's, I'm headed on a plane to Italy!"

"Oh my gosh, that's great!" I told her. "You have to tell me all about your trip."

"Absolutely," she gushed.

I led Kaylee up to my room, and she immediately pulled out her phone and started showing me pictures of her travels.

"Okay, so Paris... You *have* to come with me sometime, Cora. It's to die for," Kaylee said. "The Eiffel tower was amazing, and I met this *crazy* hot French guy who showed me around the city and took me to all these wonderful places to eat."

Kaylee continued on, telling me about all the cities she'd visited during her time abroad and the sites she'd seen. Mostly, though, she talked about the hot foreign guys.

"I got you something," she announced after finishing her stories. Kaylee reached into her purse and pulled out a little pink gift bag. I smiled at the gesture and took it from her hands.

"What is it?" I asked.

She giggled. "You'll have to open it and look inside."

I pulled open the bag, and my heart warmed. Inside was a collection of trinkets from all the countries she'd been to. I pulled each one out one by one. The first was an old statuette of the Eiffel tower. It wasn't the kind you picked up at a gift shop, either. It looked hand-crafted and had a genuine weathered look to it. I pulled out a wad of tissue paper and unrolled it to find a teacup that had the English flag on it. At the bottom of the bag was a miniature Christmas ornament of a beer stein from Germany. I drew a breath as I emptied all the contents from the bag.

Kaylee smiled proudly. "I went to every flea market I could find to get you antique souvenirs."

"Kaylee, that's so thoughtful," I said. "You didn't have to."

"Of course I did," she said simply. "You're my best friend."

I set the gifts aside on the bed, then pulled her into a hug. "Thank you. I wish I could go with you."

She tilted her head to the side. "But what about Harris Academy? It's all you've ever wanted."

I didn't really want to admit to Kaylee that it wasn't everything I dreamed. She spent years listening to me talk about how amazing life would be once I got to the academy. She'd be disappointed to hear how everything turned out.

"Yeah, it is," I said. "But it sounds like you had so much fun."

"I'm *having* a lot of fun," she reminded me. She nudged me in the side. "What's up with you? You sound… not quite like yourself."

I dropped my gaze and picked at my fingernail. "I just have a lot on my mind."

Kaylee frowned. "Is this about your semester final?"

I groaned. "You heard about that?"

Kaylee chuckled. "A Davina exposes themselves and it goes viral? Of course I'm going to hear about it."

"Oh, God." I covered my face. "Please don't tell me that's why you came home. I don't want you to stop your trip for me—"

"No," Kaylee said quickly. "Absolutely not, Cora. I've been planning this trip home for months. I just didn't tell you because I wanted to surprise you."

Kaylee crossed her legs on the bed and turned to face me. "I want to know all about your first semester."

"There's not much to tell," I admitted, though I wasn't sure that was true.

"What about your partner?" she asked. "Last time we talked, you sounded unsure of him. Did you get reassigned?"

"No," I said. "We actually worked things out. Problem is, I like him now, but he's dating this horrible girl."

With that confession, everything else just started pouring out of me. I told Kaylee all about Kellan and myself—how we couldn't get along, how I took him to the Malum portal site, how I broke his wing, and how he decided to ditch me for our final last minute. I couldn't stop talking as I recounted everything that happened during the semester final—how Celina had tried to make me fail and Kellan showed up anyway to help. It felt good to finally be saying everything out loud—and to someone I trusted.

"The Alliance threatened me, Kaylee," I said as I reached the end of my explanation. "I guess the video Kellan and I put out explaining the whole thing as a hoax satisfied them, because I haven't heard from them since. But Kaylee, I'm not sure I did the right thing."

I didn't realize I felt that way until I said it out loud.

She eyed me sideways. "What do you mean? You did what they wanted."

I bit my lower lip. "Yeah, but what if…?"

I trailed off.

"What if, what?" Kaylee asked.

"What if the Alliance is wrong?" The words felt dirty coming from my own mouth. I'd never questioned the Alliance before. They were here to protect us, to keep the Aedes and Davina a secret. People had retaliated against us before—tortured us, even. We were powerful, but not powerful enough to survive the kinds of weapons that could be used against us. That's why we had to hide in the shadows. But maybe coming out wouldn't be all bad…

Kaylee furrowed her brow. "What are you trying to say, Cora?"

I swallowed. "I've been listening to all these stories

about people who have had these amazing spiritual experiences. Maybe the people who fear us are in the minority. Maybe we can bring hope and beauty to people if they just knew the truth."

Kaylee's features hardened. "Do you really want to take that chance, Cora? People motivated by fear are… deadly."

My mouth went dry at the word *deadly*.

"Not if we fight back," I argued. "Look at the world. We're in constant war about one thing or another. It's human nature to fight. But do you know how many people have died in the name of their gods for centuries? If people knew the truth, maybe we could get along."

Kaylee eyed me cautiously, as if I'd gone insane. "Even if they knew the truth, people would deny it. You saw what everyone said about that video. The evidence was right there, and people didn't want to believe it."

"That's one video," I said. "One that was easy to explain away as false. The Aedes and Davina have years of proof that we can heal and so much evidence that we *help*."

"Yes, but you have to get people to *believe* you," Kaylee pointed out. "Cora, I'm not saying you're wrong. I'd love if we didn't have to hide who we truly are. But this isn't that simple."

My throat closed up. "The Aedes and Davina used to fight, too, Kaylee. My parents changed that. Maybe it's time we figure out a way to work alongside humans, too."

"We do work with them through the Alliance," she reminded me.

"Yeah, a *select* group of government officials," I said.

"Cora…" Kaylee trailed off, like she didn't know what else to say.

"You'd get it if you saw the kind of peace people get when they know the truth." The words slipped out before I could stop myself.

Kaylee stilled. "What are you talking about?"

My whole body tensed, and I hesitated.

"Cora." Kaylee's voice became very stern. "What do you mean?"

I couldn't hide it from Kaylee. She was my best friend, and I knew she'd pry it out of me one way or another. I lowered my voice anyway, though my parents were downstairs. "When I was in the hospital with Kellan, I showed my wings to these two little girls—"

"Oh my God, Cora!" Kaylee threw her hand over her mouth.

"Shh…" I hissed.

She dropped her voice. "You know exposing yourself is strictly forbidden!"

"I know," I said. "But these girls… one of them was sick, and—"

"So what?" Kaylee asked. "Let the other Aedes and Davina help her."

"It wasn't about healing her," I replied. "Not physically, at least. Kaylee, you should've seen her face. She was… completely at peace."

"Okay, but that's a child," Kaylee pointed out. "What about adults who are so stuck in their ways that they'll *kill* you just to maintain their own worldview?"

"I don't think that would happen—"

"Think harder!" Kaylee snapped.

I recoiled. Kaylee pressed her fingers to her eyes. After a few moments, she dropped them and looked up at me. "I'm just worried for you, Cora. I don't want you getting hurt."

"Relax, Kaylee." I reached out and placed my hand on top of hers. "I'm going to be fine."

I wasn't sure how well I could keep that promise.

5

"Are you ready for your second semester?" Dad asked brightly as the tall white boundary walls of the Harris Academy campus came into view.

Winter break had passed far too quickly, and Dad had offered to drive me back to the city. He was trying to make me feel better, but I could sense the unease in his tone. Mom hadn't come with, as she had to stay back at the restaurant.

"Ugh," I groaned, leaning against the passenger side window. "Don't ask."

He nudged me. "Everything's going to be fine, Cora. It's a new semester—a fresh start. You can put your semester final behind you."

My guts sank. Putting the past behind me was all I wanted to do, but somehow, I didn't think that was going to happen—not the way Chancellor Harris had talked about things. No matter what I did to convince the

Alliance and the rest of the world of my lie, there was no coming back from this.

Dad slowed the car to follow traffic. It was like move-in day all over again, except it felt melancholy. I wasn't excited like I used to be. The car remained quiet, as if Dad could feel my low mood in the air.

"What's going on up there?" Dad mumbled. He craned his neck to look ahead of us.

I hadn't been paying attention to the streets outside until he said something. When I looked ahead of us, I saw what was holding up traffic. My jaw tensed. People walked up and down the sidewalk holding picket signs. It wasn't like the last time I ran into the Infantry, the group that frequently protested outside campus. They'd grown in numbers, so much that there were at least a hundred people yelling obscenities as cars passed.

Barricades had been set up along the street to the academy entrance, and campus security was trying to keep all cars out who weren't faculty or students. Aedes and Davina students stood behind the barricades, as if standing guard in case a brawl broke out. My stomach dropped when I saw a face I recognized and despised.

Colt Walter stood atop a parked car and yelled into a megaphone. "They're not what they seem!" he screamed, pointing to all the cars. "They're not even human! They're demons come to steal our souls straight from our bodies."

"*We want the truth. We want the truth,*" the group chanted.

I pressed my hand to my face. "Dear God. Are they serious?"

Dad shifted his hands on the steering wheel. "If you don't want to go, you don't have to, Cora."

I hesitated as an internal battle raged inside of me. Of course I wanted to go. I still wanted to become an EMT, and nothing—not even Colt Walter and his Infantry—could stop me. I'd just like to go back knowing campus was safe.

"I'll be fine, Dad," I told him.

"Okay," he replied with a frown.

Another fifteen minutes of silence passed as we crept along the street. I sank lower and lower in my chair as we neared the line of protestors. But it didn't matter how deep I sank or how much I tried to conceal myself. As we neared the barricades, Colt Walter's eyes turned inside my vehicle, and his gaze locked on mine. His lips twisted into a sneer, and a shiver traveled down my spine.

Colt pointed straight at me. "It's her!"

My heart leapt into my throat as dozens of Infantry members started running toward our vehicle.

"Lock the car!" I shouted to my dad.

He jumped in his seat and clicked the button next to him with not a moment to spare. My pulse quickened as people surrounded our vehicle and started pounding on the windows. Dad laid on the horn, but it didn't do any good.

"Go away!" I shouted. Another useless attempt.

Colt shoved his way through the Infantry members around the car and walked straight up to my dad's window. He held his megaphone up and held it so close to the car that it almost touched the glass. "She's the demon who exposed herself!" he spat. "She's living evidence of the truth! Get out of the car and show us what you truly are!"

"I'll get out of the car and kick your fucking ass!" I screamed back at him. I could light the jackass up in flames, too—if I had an Aedes to power up my essence. Problem was, I hadn't been powered up all break, so the best I could do was knock him out. It was good enough for me, at least.

"Is that a threat?" Colt growled through the megaphone.

My hands quivered. If it were just Colt and me, I could totally take him on, but my dad and I were surrounded by so many angry people that they were starting to shake the car. Even if I wanted to fight this self-righteous asshole, I'd never get a shot at him before the rest of them took me down.

"Relax, Cora," Dad said in a calm, collected tone. "I've got this."

Dad shifted the car into park and reached for the police-issued gun on his hip. But before he could grab it, the crowd began to disperse. I didn't realize why until I saw a muscular figure step in front of Colt. He stood with his back to me and his arms crossed over his chest, looking out at the Infantry members.

"Step away from the car," he said firmly.

Kellan?

My heart lifted as more and more people like him began to surround the car, all sharing the same protective stance.

"Dad, roll your window down," I begged.

Dad frowned, but he rolled it down a crack. The cold January breeze entered the car.

"Kellan?" I called. "What are you doing?"

Kellan turned around, and my heart melted when his eyes met mine. "I've got this, partner."

Kellan turned back toward Colt. "If you want her, you're going to have to go through us to get her."

Colt's face paled momentarily, but a second later, it turned into a sneer. He glared at Kellan with pure hatred in his eyes and chuckled. "Oh, I'll get her. You just wait and see."

My mouth went dry. Colt cocked his head to the group, and the people surrounding the car dispersed. Kellan and the other supernaturals didn't move, though. They followed us along the road until we made it through the barricades. I was acutely aware of Dad's hands tightening on the steering wheel and his eyes continuously flickering down the gun on his belt.

The whole time, I couldn't stop thinking about what Colt had said.

I'll get her. You just wait and see.

He wasn't the kind of guy to just walk away. I wasn't looking forward to whatever it was he had in store for me.

6

"Cora, we need to talk."

I'd barely had a moment in my dorm before Chancellor Harris summoned me to her office. I hadn't even seen my roommate, Laura, or got the chance to unpack my suitcase.

"What's wrong?" My knees shook as I stepped into her office. It was a relief to sit in the chair across from her. Normally, I wasn't so nervous and timid, but I usually knew what to expect. Lately, surprises were being thrown at me from all directions. I had a feeling Chancellor Harris was about to throw me another one.

Chancellor Harris ignored my question and instead said, "Are you okay?"

I tucked a strand of brown hair behind my ear. "Yeah, of course. Why do you ask?"

She took a deep breath. "After everything that happened, I just wanted to make sure you're getting along well. The group outside campus hasn't hurt anyone yet, but I fear…"

She trailed off, and my stomach sank.

"You're afraid I'll be the first one?" I guessed.

She pressed her lips together and nodded. "I've seen all this happen before, Cora, and I would hate to see any one of my students get in the middle of it."

I furrowed my brow. "You've seen what happen before?"

"The fear." She swiveled her chair to look out the big window behind her desk. She stared out into the distance to the walls surrounding campus. We couldn't see the Infantry from here, but the deep, contemplating look in her eyes told me she was thinking about them.

"Years ago, the Aedes and Davina didn't get along," she said without looking at me. "We fought for millennia—all because we didn't understand each other. All because we *feared* each other. It was only when we learned that our powers worked better together that we finally declared an end to the war."

I didn't know why Chancellor Harris was telling me all this. I knew the stories well and had heard about the war first-hand from my parents, who'd been there with Chancellor Harris when it all happened. It was almost like… like she was trying to tell me something she couldn't say out loud.

I spoke slowly and deliberately, trying to decode her message. "So, if we want to prevent something like that from happening with the humans, we have to find a way to benefit everyone… But we already help them."

Chancellor Harris's eyes met mine. "They don't know that, though. And they mustn't."

I couldn't explain it, but there was something behind her eyes that conflicted with her words. Of course I knew we had to keep our existence a secret. We were outnumbered, and it was the only way to protect ourselves. Helping the humans by using our healing abilities had been a compromise with the government when they discovered what we were. They wanted to use us in war, but we wouldn't do it, and they were too afraid of us to force us. And yet, we were too afraid to expose ourselves.

Is that what our existence had come down to—fear? Were we perhaps hiding ourselves from the world because we feared what the humans would do to us? It was just a vicious cycle. One set of fear right after the other.

I hated fear. Fear was the worst of all emotions. It stopped you in your tracks. It put you at a standstill. Every other emotion drove you in one way or another, but fear halted progress all together. But right now—the way Chancellor Harris was looking at me like there was something I needed to know—fear chilled me to the bone.

I swallowed. "So, what can we do before things get out of hand?"

Chancellor Harris cleared her throat. "Well, anything we *could* do is banned by the Alliance." Chancellor Harris crossed her hands over her desk and looked to me without blinking. "Short of starting a revolution, there's nothing we can do, Cora. Understand?"

My breath stalled in my chest. Chancellor Harris was saying all the right words to keep her place as head of the academy, but there was an underlying message in her tone I couldn't deny. Chancellor Harris knew she couldn't get involved in whatever happened next, so she was asking me to do it for her.

Holy crap! Did Chancellor Harris seriously want me to start a revolution?

"I'm only a freshman, Chancellor Harris," I reminded her aloud. "Even if I wanted to do anything, I'm not cut out for it."

Her lips curled into a smirk. "Of course you wouldn't do anything, Cora. It's against Alliance laws. But don't ever underestimate yourself because of your age or experience. Need I remind you that your parents and I were younger than you are now when we closed the portal to Malum and facilitated peace among the supernatural community?"

I'd never thought of how young my parents were when they'd done all the wonderful things I'd heard about. It was crazy to think about.

Chancellor Harris looked at me in warning. "Whatever you do, Cora, I hope you will make the right choice."

I swallowed. Yeah, I hoped I did, too.

I hadn't stopped thinking about my conversation with Chancellor Harris by the time classes started on Monday.

"Are you okay?" Laura asked as we headed to the Science Building together.

I kept my face buried in my scarf. "I'm fine. Why do you ask?"

"Because you've been really quiet since we got back from break," she said.

"I'm just tired." The lie slipped out. I should've told her the truth—that I just had a lot on my mind—but I didn't know how to say it without worrying about her. I was still trying to figure out how to tell her about everything, so I decided to change the subject. "Hey, you finally got those new winter boots."

Laura opened the door to the Science Building and stomped her boots off inside the entrance. "Yeah, I got them for Christmas. Do you like them?"

She stuck her foot out to show me the black boots with fur on the top.

"I love them," I said.

"My class is this way." Laura pointed down the hall. "I'll see you at lunch. We're going to talk about this then, okay?"

I nodded. I knew I couldn't keep all this from Laura much longer. "See you."

Laura and I waved goodbye to each other. I headed in the opposite direction of her toward my Intermediate Firefighting class. My gut sank when I stepped into the room and saw Kellan and Celina sitting up front. He had an arm draped over the back of her chair and was leaned in close to her. He brushed her short hair away from her ear and whispered something into it. She giggled in a way that made me want to hurl.

Kellan caught my eye as I passed by their table. He hesitated, like he wasn't sure whether to sit next to me—his partner—or Celina—his girlfriend. Celina's laughter instantly died, and she shot me daggers. I breezed past their table and took a seat in the back. Kellan shot me a look of apology, and I forced a smile back. I'd be lying if I said I wasn't disappointed that he didn't want to work with me in this class.

Professor Taylor and Professor Arnold entered the room a few moments later. They were the same teaching pair who taught our Intro to Firefighting class last semester.

"Welcome back, students!" Professor Arnold said at the front of the room. He was in a good mood like always.

"Before we begin, I'd like to congratulate you all on passing your first semester final."

At the front of the room, Celina scoffed. She glanced in my direction and mumbled something under her breath. I couldn't hear her from here, but I was pretty sure it was along the lines of, "*Some* of us passed."

My lips tightened. Did she not realize she was insulting her boyfriend right in front of him? I wasn't the only one who'd failed.

"You've all come a long way and have proven you have what it takes to continue in the program," Professor Arnold continued. "This semester, we'll be diving into more advanced tactics for controlling fires and new scenarios with your essence. Let's get started."

I still had my eyes on Celina and Kellan. Kellan said something I didn't hear. Celina placed a gentle hand on his shoulder and replied, "Oh, no. Not you. I know what happened wasn't your fault."

Her comment was laughable. When you really thought about it, it was all Celina's fault.

Kellan approached me in the hall after class. "Hey, Cora."

I stopped in my tracks and glanced around, expecting Celina to be attached to his side, but she was headed off toward another class in the opposite direction.

"What is it, Kellan?" I snapped without meaning to. "Come to insult me some more?"

His brow furrowed deeply. "Insult you?"

"Isn't that what you and Celina were doing the whole lecture?" I accused.

I pressed my lips together. I didn't want to fight with Kellan. It would only make the whole situation worse. Besides, he wasn't the problem. His girlfriend was.

Kellan sighed. "Come on, Cora. She didn't mean it. She's just upset because I got hurt."

"Why are you making excuses for her?" I asked.

Kellan frowned. "Look, I'll talk to her, okay?"

I relaxed a little. "So, what do you need?"

"I was wondering if you wanted to get lunch together," he said.

My whole body tensed. "You—you want to get lunch with me?"

"Well, yeah," he replied simply. "We're partners." He paused a moment before adding, "Wait. We're not still fighting, are we?"

I let out a light chuckle. "After everything that happened? No."

"Oh, good." He pressed his hand to his heart for show.

Damn it. It was hard not to like him when he wasn't acting like a jerk all the time.

I didn't say anything while we walked, and the silence was awkward. Kellan must've noticed, because he stopped just inside the front doors.

"Cora?" he asked. "Are you okay?"

I was still getting used to him showing concern for me, and it made my head spin every time.

I pushed a strand of dark hair behind my ear. "Okay? Of course I'm okay."

"You don't seem like yourself," he observed. "It's like you have something on your mind."

Only everything.

"Is this about that Colt guy?" Kellan asked.

I shook my head. "No, but thanks again for stepping in."

Kellan smirked. "Hey, I'm your partner. It's what I'm here for."

I raised a playful eyebrow. "Protecting me from weirdos? Because you've done that more than once."

I still hadn't forgotten how Kellan had shown up last semester when the Infantry attacked Laura and me outside the academy.

Kellan shrugged. "I've gotta protect my own. Who would I heal with if I didn't have you?"

My heart lifted in my chest while he spoke, then quickly plummeted at the last comment. I knew he didn't mean it like that, but it sounded like he was only keeping me around so he could pass his classes.

"Aw, you're such a sweetheart," I teased as I punched him lightly on the shoulder. Inside, a rock had settled in my gut. "The truth is, Kellan, I have something I need to talk to you about."

Kellan glanced around at the people coming in and out of the building. He cocked his head, and I followed him into an empty classroom. He closed the door behind us and turned to me. I was surprised by the deep look of concern in his features.

"What's wrong, Cora?" he asked, like he genuinely cared.

I took a deep breath and clutched the strap of my bag tighter. "Chancellor Harris and I spoke."

Kellan furrowed his brow, as if wondering where this was going. "About what?"

"Well, about…" I pressed my lips together. "It's hard to explain, because she didn't really *say* anything to me."

"What do you mean?" he questioned.

"It was like… like she was trying to send me a silent message," I admitted. "She said she worried that the Infantry was going to hurt me, but that there was nothing we could do about it. But then she started talking about how she and my parents closed the portal to Malum and how they were younger than me. It was like she wanted me to take action somehow."

Kellan considered my words. "Take action?"

"Yeah, like try to make peace with the Infantry or something," I said. "Kellan, I think she wants us to reveal ourselves."

Kellan's features fell, and the muscles in his jaw tightened. "No, Cora. You must've misread her."

I crossed my arms. "I don't think I did."

"You've heard Chancellor Harris say it a million times—keeping our secret is vital," Kellan pointed out. "Besides, the Alliance would have you arrested. Why would you want to reveal yourself after you just covered up the last incident?"

I thought back to the girls in the hospital room, but I didn't mention them to Kellan. "I think the truth will bring people peace, Kellan."

"You can't make that decision for everyone," he shot back.

I ran my fingers through my hair, trying to find the words that could explain how I felt. "Look, I... I..." I didn't even know where to start.

Kellan raised an eyebrow, waiting for my explanation.

I sighed. "I used to think all that mattered was getting through school and shit like that, but life is so much more complicated."

"You're right," he said bluntly. "It is."

A silent beat passed where we just stared at each other. I didn't expect him to agree with me.

Kellan breathed a deep sigh. "But exposing ourselves, Cora... That only makes things *more* complicated."

"For a while, maybe," I agreed. "But once things settle down—"

"How do you know they'll settle down?" he interrupted, taking on a harsher tone.

I gaped at him. "I just have to trust that they will."

Kellan started pacing through the classroom. "You have to remember history, Cora."

"I know my history," I shot back.

He raked his fingers through his hair and turned back to me. "Then you'll remember when we were kids and that story about the people who captured those Aedes and ripped their wings off."

I swallowed. "I remember the story."

"Right, but do you *feel* it?" he asked harshly.

My voice became small. "What do you mean?"

"Have you ever felt the persecution for what you are?" Kellan repeated. "Do you have even the slightest idea what it'd be like if you exposed yourself?"

I wanted to tell him about how I showed myself to the girls in the hospital, but he was so worked up that I couldn't do it. My heart sank.

"You have no idea, Cora," he said through clenched teeth, like he was trying not to freak out on me. The truth was, he was scaring me. There was a look in his eyes I'd never seen before, one that chilled me to the bone. I didn't know what it meant. "Before you go exposing yourself, think of how it would affect everyone else."

I opened myself to reply, but my phone began ringing in my pocket, cutting me off. I grabbed it and saw my dad was calling. I turned my gaze to Kellan before I answered. "I'm not trying to be selfish, Kellan. I'm trying to do what's best for everyone."

I punched the screen on my phone and turned away from him. "Hey, Dad. What's up?"

"Cora?" he asked breathlessly.

My stomach plummeted to my toes. I could instantly tell by the sound of his voice something was wrong.

"I'm here. What is it?" I demanded.

"Where are you, Cora?" Dad asked. "Are you safe?"

Kellan heard my father through the phone, and his features instantly softened. He stared at me wide-eyed.

"Yeah, Dad. I'm fine," I answered. "I'm with Kellan at school."

Dad breathed a sigh of relief. "I'm so glad to hear that."

"Why, Dad?" I pressed. He was really starting to freak me out. "What's wrong?"

The line went silent for a moment, until Dad took a big breath. "It's the restaurant, Cora. There's been an explosion."

The room spun around me. I was sure my father was saying something more, but I couldn't process it. Mom's restaurant was gone? The business she built from the ground up? Our family's prime source of income? Her very passion?

I could hardly wrap my head around it. I'd spent so many summers there, coloring in the booth in the corner or helping fold napkins in the back. How could something like this happen?

Minutes must've passed, but it felt like a lifetime. I sank into one of the seats at the front of the empty classroom. Kellan grabbed my phone from my hand and started talking to my dad.

"Mister Marek," he said.

Dad replied to him, but I didn't hear what he said. I was still trying to make sense of what my father had said. How could my mother's beautiful restaurant be reduced to nothing by my very own element? I wished I'd been there to put out the flames. Hell, why didn't my dad do it? He had fire essence the same as me.

They exchanged a few more words I couldn't process.

"Are you sure it can't be salvaged?" Kellan asked my father.

I snapped back to attention, curious to hear his answer.

"The building's too far gone," Dad said. "They suspect some sort of accelerant was used, but they're also considering the possibility of a gas leak. We won't know more until the investigation concludes."

"Was anyone hurt?" I blurted. "Where's Mom?"

"Shh…" Kellan said, listening closely to my dad. "Okay. We'll be there as soon as we can."

Kellan hung up, and I gaped at him.

"Why did you do that!?" I yelled as I shot up out of my chair. "I had more questions."

"I'll tell you in the car." Kellan grabbed my elbow and dragged me out of the room.

I pulled against him. "No, Kellan! Stop!"

He dropped my arm, but his lips tightened in anger when he looked at me. "Look, do you want to go home and see your parents or not?"

I planted my feet firmly in place. I didn't care that there were a group of people passing by. I wasn't moving until Kellan gave me answers. "Tell me what my dad said."

Kellan pushed his hand through his hair. "Your mom's going to make it, but—"

"Oh God!" My hand shot over my mouth. I didn't like the way he said that. It wasn't good at all.

Kellan placed his hands on my shoulders to get me to calm down. "*But…* she was badly burned."

Tears pricked at my eyes. "How bad? Will they be able to heal her?"

"They're working on it as we speak," Kellan told me.

I dropped my shaking hand. "What else did my dad say?"

"He wanted you to stay here at the academy."

"No. No way," I replied. I started walking briskly toward the door. "I'm going to see my mom."

"I knew you'd say that," Kellan said as he fell into step beside me. "Which is why I told your dad we're going to Eagle Valley. I'm taking you. I'm not letting you do this alone."

My chest twisted into knots as I thought of what my mother must be going through right now. But when Kellan said that, the knot eased ever so slightly.

We hurried out of the Science Building and to the parking lot. The cold wind bit at my nose, and my hands shook as I reached for the passenger-side door of Kellan's black sedan.

Kellan drove out of the academy gates. The street was empty, save for a few cars passing along.

It was an hour drive back to Eagle Valley, and it must've been the longest hour of my life. I had no idea what sort of condition my mother was in, and I was imagining the worst. Even with essence to heal and powers of her own, burns were dangerous. If they burnt through layers of skin, it took great care to heal each layer.

Kellan glanced to me from the driver's seat the closer

we got to Eagle Valley. "Cora, please say something. You haven't talked the whole ride."

I kept my eyes on the landscape out of the window. This area was home, but it didn't feel right. I swallowed the lump in my throat. "I'm scared, Kellan."

"Your mom will be fine," he assured me. "Your dad said—"

"That's not the only thing I'm scared of," I admitted.

"Then what, Cora?" he begged. "Whatever it is, you can tell me."

"I know," I said in a small voice. He was my partner. We were supposed to trust each other, but I just couldn't bear to say what I was thinking out loud. I took a deep breath and forced the words out. "I'm scared because I'm afraid someone did this on purpose."

Kellan pressed his lips together. He didn't answer right away, like he was wondering the same thing.

"My dad basically admitted it," I pointed out. "He said an accelerant might've been used. Kellan, what if this was my fault?"

"No!" He slammed his hand against the steering wheel, which made me jump. "Don't say that."

"But it's a real possibility," I argued. "Nothing like this has ever happened to my family. Now my mom's restaurant burns down days after Colt Walter threatened me."

A shadow fell over Kellan's face. "Even if he did this, you can't blame yourself. You're not the one who started the fire."

Kellan's words should've reassured me, but they didn't. My pulse quickened the closer we got to my hometown. By the time we entered the outskirts of town near Galen High School, my heart was hammering against my chest.

"Are you sure you want to see this?" Kellan asked me softly.

I closed my eyes and nodded. "This is what I'm going to school for."

"Cora, this isn't some class assignment," he reminded me. "This is personal."

My hands knotted in my lap. "I know. I can handle it."

I wasn't lying, but I also wasn't prepared for what I was about to see. Ahead, Main Street was blocked off by a *Road Closed* sign. All I saw were the barricades and a huge crowd of onlookers. Kellan parked along the street as close as we could get. I jumped out of the car before he even shut the car off.

I sprinted toward the intersection—and my feet halted beneath me when I rounded the corner. Time seemed to stand still as an invisible knife pierced my stomach and gutted me.

Behind all the emergency response vehicles and flashing lights of police cars, Mom's restaurant was nothing more than a charred memory of what it once was. The fire had already been put out, but it was like I was still watching it burn. I didn't even recognize the restaurant, and I'd never know what the building was if it hadn't been there my whole life. The roof had completely caved in, and the sign that read *Cozy Cafe* was nowhere to be seen. Anywhere that wasn't charred to bits had soot all over it. The businesses that sandwiched my mom's restaurant had experienced minimal damage. It was clear that whoever had done this had intentionally targeted my mom.

My gaze darted around the area, searching for any signs of my parents. My eyes fell on my dad next to the other police officers. He was in his usual police gear and was talking to his deputy.

"Dad!" I cried as I raced over to him.

The officer who was trying to keep people away from the area let me pass.

Dad turned in my direction. He looked relieved to see me. "Cora."

I slammed into him, throwing my arms around his neck. Dad hugged me back tightly. He ran his fingers through my hair as I buried my face into his shoulder. The smell of smoke filled my nostrils, and tears began to stream down my face.

I heard Kellan come up beside us, but I didn't want him to see me cry, so I wiped the tears into my dad's shoulder and put on a mask as I drew away from him. The longer I held it, the tighter the knot in my chest became.

"Dad, where's Mom?" I demanded. "How bad is it?"

"Cora, calm down," Dad insisted, placing a hand on my shoulder. He held on tight, like he couldn't contain his anger. "Your mother is in good hands."

"Why aren't you with her?" I cried.

Dad's lips tightened. He was always trying to play the hero. I knew why he wasn't with Mom, though he wouldn't say it. He wanted to catch the bastard who did this to her.

"How did this happen?" I demanded. "How many people were hurt?"

Dad shot a glance to the other officers, then guided me away. Kellan was polite and didn't follow.

Dad took a deep breath. "Everyone else got out when the fire started. Your mom…"

My hands shot over my mouth. "What'd she do?"

Both of my parents sort of had a hero complex. Mom was almost too kind-hearted for her own good.

A muscle in dad's jaw popped. "Your mom went back inside to save her recipes moments before the explosion."

"Oh my God!" I cried. "Why doesn't she keep those on a damn computer like a normal person?"

"Well, they came from Grandma Gloria, and—"

"I don't care!" I shouted. "She could've been killed."

Dad's tone softened. "Do you want to go see her?"

"No, Dad," I said sarcastically while wiping tears from my eyes. "That's not why I came all the way home."

Dad frowned, but he didn't reprimand me for my sarcasm. "Okay, let's go."

Dad started leading me toward his police cruiser. Kellan stopped me before I could get in the car.

"Hey, Cora," he said softly. "You take all the time you need. I'll be here for you when you get back."

"Wait," I replied. "You're not coming?"

"This stuff with your mom is private," he told me. "Go visit her."

My stomach sank. "You don't have to wait around."

Kellan frowned. "How are you going to get back to the academy."

Right. I glanced to my dad, who was climbing into the driver's seat. "I'll get my dad to drive me back.

Thanks for driving me, Kellan. And just... being here for me."

"Of course." Kellan reached out and wiped a tear from my eye before I even realized it had formed. We both stilled at the contact.

Kellan cleared his throat and broke the silence. "You should go."

I didn't feel like I could leave him like that. Before I knew what I was doing, I threw my arms around his neck and squeezed him into a tight hug. He tensed for a moment, then relaxed as he hugged me back. It was weird for us, but somehow, it also felt natural.

I drew away from Kellan, though I didn't want to. "Really, Kellan. Thank you."

At that, I turned around and climbed into my dad's cruiser. "Let's go see Mom."

I stepped into the hospital with a heavy sense of dread in my stomach. The nurse pointed us in the direction of Mom's room. I pushed the door open, and my heart stalled in my chest.

Mom lay on the bed with bandages covering her arms and legs. Burn marks marred her face, and patches of hair were missing. It was obvious they'd already tried healing some of it, but I couldn't imagine it looking any worse.

Mom's eyes darted to Dad and me when we entered, but she didn't move. It was so bad she could hardly show emotion on her face.

"Cora," she breathed, like she was relieved, though her voice came out strained.

"Oh my God, Mom," I whispered as I stepped into the room. I stopped at her bedside and ran my hands lightly over the bandages. "It's bad…"

"I'll be okay," Mom said, but I didn't know how she did it when she looked like this.

I sniffled. "I know you can heal, but to be in that kind of pain in the first place…"

I looked down to her arms, though I tried not to picture what was beneath the bandages. Mom must've noticed my expression because she rushed to explain. "I'm not going to lie to you, Cora. There are some deep burns. The healers have already taken care of the minor ones, but the others they'll have to do in stages. I'm less worried about the injuries and more worried about the restaurant."

I scoffed. That was such a Mom thing to say.

"Ryn," Dad said to her sternly. "You need to worry about healing. Forget about the restaurant."

Mom pressed her lips together. "That restaurant is my life, Marek."

"And the insurance will pay for it." Dad took her face gently in his hands and tried to reassure her. "We'll get through this, Ryn."

Dad pressed a kiss to Mom's forehead. She swallowed as he drew away.

"At least I still have you two," she whispered, looking at us both longingly.

The lump in my throat grew bigger. "Mom, I'm so sorry."

"Don't be," she said gently. "It's not your fault."

I shook my head. "You don't know that."

"What do you mean, Cora?" Dad demanded. "You don't think those people from the academy had anything to do with this?"

I turned my gaze up to Dad. "I don't know. It's too big of a coincidence. If someone wanted to hurt me and couldn't get inside the academy, what do you think their next move would be?"

Mom's lips turned down at the corners, but it looked like it pained her. "Going after our family restaurant. Cora…"

"I know I don't have any evidence," I said. "And you may never catch the guy who did this. But something deep in my gut says this is about me."

Dad pressed his lips together. "They're afraid of you," he said thoughtfully.

"No." I shook my head. "This isn't the kind of thing someone does out of fear. Whoever did this—and I think I know who—they did it out of anger."

And that was the most dangerous motive of all.

After the fire, I didn't feel like myself. Every now and then, I'd forget that anything had happened, and then it came rushing back like a tidal wave. Colt Walter had hurt my family. That wasn't something I could easily forgive.

I hoped that the justice system would run its course, but according to Dad, Colt Walter had a rock solid alibi backed up by his Infantry group. I was shocked at first, but then I started to wonder if Colt had somehow fabricated the alibi. As for suspects, they had none, which seemed awfully fishy to me considering Dad basically admitted it was arson.

At this point, I didn't know what to do. Chancellor Harris wanted me to fight back, but Kellan wasn't on board, and neither was Laura.

"Kellan's right," she told me. "Exposing ourselves will only get you arrested by the Alliance."

"They didn't arrest me last time," I reminded her.

She frowned. "What will happen on your second

offence? They won't forgive you again, Cora. You won't get a second chance to explain it away. I'm not sure I get what you hope to accomplish."

Laura's words felt harsh at the time, but the more I thought on it, the more I wondered if she was right. Even when I exposed myself at my semester final, people wrote it off as unbelievable. Perhaps they'd never believe what was right in front of them, no matter how many times I showed them.

But Laura hadn't seen those young girls' faces at the hospital. She didn't know what it felt like to be someone else's source of hope. All I wanted was for everyone else to feel that sense of peace.

I tried to put it out of my mind, but it kept creeping back in even weeks later. I was sitting alone in the Clark Hall rec room, going over my human physiology homework, when the sound of a child's voice came over the TV. I looked up to see a young girl with pretty curls and chocolate eyes staring back at me. She was standing outside in the snow with a thick coat wrapped around her, and she was talking to someone beyond the camera. She held something in her hand, though I couldn't see what it was.

Saddie?

"It was my sister's idea," she told the interviewer. "She wanted everyone at school to know that even if they're bullied or they feel bad sometimes, they're not alone. All the kids will see the tree when they're walking into school, so they remember all day that everything's going to be okay."

The camera angle shifted, and it showed this large,

beautiful evergreen growing at the front of one of the local schools. Hundreds of angel-wing ornaments hung from the branches. Names had been scribbled across each one in permanent marker—one for each student at Becca and Saddie's school.

My heart warmed.

The camera shifted back to Saddie. "I think if my sister were here right now, she'd be really proud. She never got to see the tree, but she would've loved it."

My stomach dropped. Becca was gone?

The news hit me like a bulldozer. If I hadn't been sitting, I'd have been knocked off my feet.

Gone...

No, she wasn't gone forever. Her essence was out there. That peace she'd found had inspired her to create this angel tree for her classmates. Her legacy lived on.

Something sparked in my heart at the realization. I barely knew what I was doing when I jumped up from the couch and shoved my textbook in my bag. All I knew was that I had to see Becca one last time. I had to witness the legacy she left behind.

I ran back to my room to drop off my homework and pick up my jacket. Laura wasn't around, since she was in her elementals class. I threw on my jacket and tightened my scarf around my neck as I left the dorm hall. I left out the back gate to the academy and walked the next block to the bus stop.

What am I doing?

The thought crossed my mind while I was waiting, then

I wondered why I even questioned it in the first place. I shouldn't be ashamed of this. I couldn't turn back.

I rode the bus all the way across town, until it came close enough to the school that I could walk the rest of the way. I shivered at the cold winter air on my skin, but I didn't slow down. My heart pounded the closer I got…

And then I saw it, and everything stilled.

My heart slowed, and even the wind seemed to die down. A beautiful warmth surrounded me as I stopped across the street from the school and looked up at Becca's angel tree. The clouds parted, and sunlight shone down on the tree. The white angel wing ornaments twisted and turned in a beautiful, sparkling display. It was as if I could feel Becca's essence around the tree, sharing her message of peace and beauty.

The street was eerily quiet. It was so unusual that it snapped me back to attention. I looked both ways, then crossed the street to the angel tree. I stopped when I got close enough to touch it. I pulled my glove off and reached out to run my fingers over the nearest ornament. It was strangely warm, considering the chilly weather. As the ornament twisted around, the name written on it came into view.

Becca.

I inhaled a sharp breath. It was like a message from Becca herself, though I didn't know what it meant.

Moments later, the sound of a diesel engine met my ears, pulling me out of my trance. I glanced down the street to see a line of school busses driving toward the school. They turned into the parking lot and stopped next to the front doors. I didn't realize how late it was already, but it must've been time for school to let out.

I didn't pay much attention to the kids flooding out of the school and onto the busses. I kept my gaze on the angel ornaments, reading each name. I didn't know exactly what I was looking for. I hoped to see Saddie's name, but each name I read filled me with a warm, fuzzy sensation. It was like the entire tree was a list of the people Becca had inspired.

"It's you again!"

A familiar voice caught my attention. I turned to see Saddie letting go of an older man's hand and running in my direction.

A smile broke across my face when I saw her. "Hey, how are you?" I asked.

Saddie spread her arms and threw them around me, squeezing me tight.

"Whoa," I chuckled, totally caught off guard.

"I'm so glad you made it," she said as she pulled away from me.

"What do you mean?" I asked.

Saddie looked up to me with bright eyes. "Becca wanted you to see it," she stated simply.

"Me?" I balked.

Saddie nodded. "She made it because of you."

I couldn't get what Saddie had said out of my mind.

She made it because of you.

Becca had died, and her last wish was to inspire others —because of me. The idea had totally floored me. I'd never been an inspiration to anyone.

And maybe it was because I'd always had to hide who I was.

I still hadn't mentioned it to Laura or Kellan. I didn't know how to tell them that I'd shown my wings to those two girls. But the guilt at keeping my secret was eating away at me. A heavy rock seemed to settle in my gut over the next few weeks, and every time I opened my mouth, it was as if my throat was closing up. I feared that the secret might slip out before I could stop it, and I knew nothing good could come of it.

"Cora?" Kellan nudged me in the side.

I snapped back to attention. We were sitting in our Art

of Healing II lab, and Professor Kovski had just finished giving instructions on how to use our essence to diagnose internal issues. Each of the rats placed in front of us had some sort of internal anomaly, and we were supposed to spend the lab diagnosing them.

I swallowed the lump in my throat. "Sorry. I just spaced out a second. Let's get started."

Kellan looked down to the paper that'd been handed to us with our rat. "Symptoms include limping and low appetite."

"That's it?" I asked.

Kellan nodded. "Do you want to try looking inside?"

"Sure." I took a deep breath as Kellan placed his hand on my shoulder. He held my shoulder so many times throughout the past few months, and it was still like an electric shock every time he made contact—and it wasn't from his power, either.

Kellan drew my essence into himself, and power rushed through me as my essence channel opened wider. I let it flow into him for several moments before turning my attention to the sedated rat. I placed my hands over the creature and closed my eyes. I pushed a small amount of essence into his body. My magic explored the rat's body effortlessly. As I turned my focus to its legs, I felt my magic pushing back and resisting me.

"I can feel an injury in the left leg," I told Kellan.

"Perfect," he said. "Any idea what it is?"

I honed my attention on the leg, but no matter how hard I pushed, I couldn't pinpoint which tissue had been affected or how severe the injury was.

"Whoa!" Kellan grabbed my hands and yanked them away from the rat.

My eyes shot open. "What's wrong?"

Kellan stared back at me with knitted eyebrows, like he was trying hard to read my expression. "We're not supposed to heal them, Cora. The assignment is just to diagnose them."

"I wasn't trying to heal it," I told him.

He raised his eyebrows. "Your hands started to glow."

I glanced down to them. I'd never healed without purposely trying to. "I didn't mean to."

Kellan pressed his fingers to his eyes. "Cora, what's going on?"

I recoiled a bit. "What do you mean?"

He sighed and dropped his hands. Next to us, Caleb and Shaylene cried out in victory as they diagnosed their rat with a digestive disorder. No one was paying attention to Kellan and me, but he lowered his voice anyway.

"Your head's been all over the place lately," Kellan said gently.

A few months ago, I'd have been offended by his statement, but I knew now Kellan was only saying it to help me. He wasn't exactly wrong, either.

"We need to talk about what's going on," he stated. "If this is about your mom, you know you can borrow my car to go see her. Or better yet, I'll drive you."

That weight in my gut seemed to lift slightly at the generous offer, but it quickly settled back in when I reminded myself I was hiding things from him.

"No, Kellan," I said. "It's not about my mom. I've talked

to her. She's doing better, and she says not to worry. It's about…"

I glanced around the room. Though no one was listening to us, I didn't feel comfortable talking about this out in the open.

"It's about something else," I settled on.

Kellan eyed me curiously. "Something you're going to talk to me about? Because as your partner—"

"I know," I said, cutting him off. "I know. Partners need to work together. And be honest with each other. And I want to. I just…"

I took a deep breath. "I'll tell you after class."

"Okay," Kellan agreed.

We turned back to our rat, but now my mind was so consumed with how to tell Kellan that I couldn't concentrate on the assignment. I expected Kellan to push me, but he kept quiet and waited patiently.

By the time class ended, I could tell he was about to burst with impatience. He grabbed his bag and practically pushed me out of the classroom.

"So, what is it you want to tell me?" he asked once we were out in the hall.

I bit my lower lip. "It's not really something I can tell you. I have to show you."

Kellan didn't seem too keen on the idea of being kept in the dark, but he seemed really curious. We got in his car, and I pointed him in the direction of the elementary school.

When we reached the angel tree, I pointed to the curb. "Right here's fine."

Kellan pulled over and parked the car. He glanced up and down the street, until his eyes finally fell on the sparkling ornaments in the front of the school lawn.

"This is what you wanted to show me?" he asked. "What is it?"

I steadied my hands in my lap. "There's something I need to tell you, but you have to promise me you won't freak out."

He eyed me up and down, and his lips pressed into a thin line. "I'm not making any promises."

There was the Kellan I knew.

"Let's just say I don't need a lecture on this, okay?" I said. "It'll only make it worse."

The curiosity in Kellan's features deepened. "Cora, what's going on?"

I didn't know why I was so scared to tell anyone—but Kellan especially.

All my life, it'd been ingrained in me that exposing myself was among one of the worst things a supernatural could do—that if you exposed yourself, you exposed everyone. Though a part of me questioned it, another part of me still believed it was true. I felt like I'd failed everyone—Kellan, Kaylee, Laura, my parents... I felt like a sinner.

And yet, I felt like I'd done the right thing. It didn't make any sense.

I took a deep breath. "A few weeks ago when you were in the hospital, something happened."

Kellan's hands tightened on the steering wheel. "With that Alliance guy? John Maddox?"

"No," I said quickly, though Kellan didn't relax. If anything, the shadow over his face darkened.

"Then what?" he asked firmly.

"I met these girls," I said. "They were young, and they'd just been in a car accident. One of them had an immune disease—the kind of thing we can't heal."

Kellan didn't say anything. He just sat there and listened, which almost felt worse than if he'd said something by now.

"Anyway, the girls… they recognized me, and it was like… like they wanted me to be real. Like they needed a real angel in their lives," I admitted.

Kellan's eyes widened as he realized where I was going with this. "Cora, you didn't—"

"I showed them my wings," I spat out.

Kellan's eyes widened, and his knuckles turned white on the steering wheel. His lips pressed so thin I could barely see them.

"Are you serious, Cora?" Kellan demanded.

His tone was harsh, but he didn't move.

"I am," I stated firmly.

Kellan raked his fingers through his hair, though he didn't look at me. He kept his gaze out the front window. "Cora, you *know* what exposing ourselves could do!"

"I know, but Kellan—"

He finally turned to me, his eyes dark. "People get hurt when this kind of stuff happens," he growled.

My heart rate spiked. Kellan and I had fought before, but I'd never seen him look so angry.

"God, Cora," Kellan huffed. "You were *just* let off for

exposing yourself once. You got lucky. If the Alliance finds out about this, they'll arrest you."

"I know," I said. "You don't think I've already considered that?"

Kaylee had made sure I knew it when I talked to her about this.

"But so what?" I continued. "Let them arrest me. I wouldn't take back what I did."

"That's because you didn't get hurt!" Kellan roared.

I drew away from him, pressing myself up against the passenger-side door. His tone was so harsh, it was like he was taking this too personally.

Kellan shook his head and looked out his window, then mumbled under his breath. "It's no wonder the Infantry is after you."

My jaw dropped. "*Excuse* me?"

Kellan's nostrils flared as he turned back to me. "You heard me. What you did was reckless, Cora. If the Infantry wants to make an example out of the supernaturals, they were smart to choose you."

I crossed my arms. "That's low, Kellan."

He shrugged. "It's true."

I narrowed my eyes at him. I was about ready to step out of the car and walk back to campus myself. I thought Kellan and I had gotten over all this fighting. I thought I could confide in him. "You haven't even heard everything I want to say."

"Do I want to?" he asked. "You can't just go around exposing yourself, Cora."

"I exposed myself to save you!" I yelled.

"Yeah, the first time," he shot back. "What's your reasoning for the second? And how are you going to justify the one after that? And after that? When people get hurt, how are you going to justify that, Cora? What about your mom? Tell me how you justify that."

A lump rose to my throat. I could hardly get the words out. "I'm not the one who started that fire."

"You started it the moment you flew out of that burning building," he accused.

A piercing stab like a knife to the gut tore through me. I couldn't stop the next words from flying out of my mouth. "Would you rather I'd have left you there to die!?"

The car went dead silent, but it was the loudest silence I'd ever heard. My ears rang, and the words I'd just spoken echoed in my mind. *I'd have left you there to die...*

Kellan glared at me, but his tone finally softened. "I don't know, Cora. To protect the supernatural community, maybe you should've."

Tears welled in my eyes. Kellan would prefer to die than expose himself?

Kellan's hands shook in his lap, but he wouldn't look at me. "You don't get it, Cora. You've never felt what it's like to be persecuted for what you are."

He was *not* using the Aedes card on me.

"You mean because you're Aedes and I'm Davina?" I accused.

"No," he said simply. "You grew up surrounded by people who were just like you. You didn't have to worry about exposing yourself, because you got to do it wherever you went without repercussions."

"You did, too," I reminded him. "You went to a super-natural high school, too."

Kellan nodded. When he looked at me, his expression had softened. It was so full of sorrow that my heart became filled with compassion for him—and I didn't even know why.

"It wasn't always like that, though," Kellan said. "I'm only half Aedes. Remember?"

After a beat of silence, he continued. "I grew up between two worlds—the human world, where anyone could be what they wanted and the only secrets were where you hid your candy after Halloween, and the super-natural world, where I was forbidden from speaking to anyone about what I was. I didn't really know which world I belonged in. I didn't know how to tell a human from a supernatural. Hell, I still barely know the difference."

"Kellan," I said softly, but he cut me off.

"When I was eight, I went to a sleepover at this kid's house. There were four of us upstairs playing video games. One of my friends asked the other when his dad was coming home, and he said he wasn't. When we asked him why, he said, *'Because he's an angel.'*"

My breath stalled. I didn't know where Kellan's story was going, but the way he spoke, it didn't sound like it was going anywhere good.

Kellan continued. "To eight-year-old ears that had really only heard the term used for Davina, I was obviously concerned. I thought he meant his dad worked an impor-tant Davina job and was gone from home a lot. So when the other two boys left the room, I confronted my friend. I told him it was against the rules to tell people his dad was an angel. He didn't have any clue what I was talking about. I thought he was just playing along, you know. So I said the Aedes and Davina had to be kept a secret. He still said he didn't know what I meant, so I told him we didn't have to lie to each other anymore because I was Aedes. He *still* didn't know what I meant."

Kellan pressed his hand to his temple, like looking back on the memory was particularly stressful for him. "I should've just stopped there, but in my little kid mind, I was convinced my friend was a Davina. When he asked what an Aedes was, I remember saying, *'I'm Aedes. If your dad's an angel, you must've heard of us.'* He asked if an Aedes was some sort of guardian angel. I told him I was just like his dad with black wings, so he asked me to show him."

Oh, shit. I knew now where Kellan's story was going.

"I should've realized at that point that he only meant his father was dead, but I couldn't see past my excitement for meeting another boy my age who knew about our supernatural gifts," Kellan said. "And so I showed him my wings. It was the biggest mistake of my life. The other two boys walked in just then. The three of them took one look at my wings and began chanting *demon.* The first insisted that I was nothing like his father, that my wings must be black because I was evil. They dragged me outside in the rain where his mom couldn't hear and beat me to a pulp. I remember crying and shivering beneath a cold downpour, wondering where I went wrong and how my friends could turn on me so quickly. I realize now that they were frightened of me and took to hurting me before I could hurt them, but at the time, I just thought they were cruel. I stumbled several blocks home in the rain. I could barely see past my swollen eyes. Each raindrop was a needle of pain on my tender cheeks."

I pressed my hand to my mouth, and my eyes burned at the threat of tears. I had no idea Kellan had gone through something so horrible.

"When I got home, I told my mom the fight had been over a video game, but sometimes I wonder if she sensed the truth," Kellan admitted. "She transferred me to a new school that fall, and I never saw those boys again. I've never told anyone this story until now."

A single tear streaked my face. "Kellan," I whispered. "I'm so sorry you went through that."

He stared out the front window. "I don't want that to happen to any other kid like me. I want them to know what to say in those kinds of situations, be taught how to handle it. That's why I wanted to be part of the Alliance."

"You're right, Kellan," I said. "That should never happen to any other kid. And that's why I think it's worth telling people, so we can educate them, so they don't have to be afraid."

Kellan shook his head. "You don't want to take that risk, Cora."

"Kellan, I already showed two girls what I am, and it inspired them," I told him. "That tree right there was made by these girls for the other kids, so they could walk into school every day with a guardian watching over them."

Kellan shot me a skeptical look. "Guardian angels aren't real, Cora."

"So what?" I challenged. "All that matters is if the kids believe it."

"And would they if you told them the truth?" Kellan asked. "Cora, I'm sorry, but a few ornaments that will be taken down in a month are nothing compared to what happened to me."

My jaw dropped. "I'm not saying it is. But if we can inspire people—"

"We can scare people, too," he reminded me. "The world isn't ready for this."

"The world will never be ready!" I argued. "And yet accidents keep happening. We continue to reveal ourselves despite the laws. The Alliance can't keep covering it up and locking people away forever."

"But they can," he insisted. "The Davina have been doing it for millennia."

"Kellan, you don't understand—"

"No, Cora," he said firmly. "*You* don't understand. If you think I'm going to support you in this, the answer is no."

It was clear Kellan wasn't budging on this issue. Which meant that somehow, someway, I was going to have to find another way to solve this.

My talk with Kellan didn't exactly go as I expected, but the outcome was essentially the same—he freaked out and still thought it was a bad idea to expose ourselves. Telling Laura the truth, at least, was a little easier to handle.

"I have a confession to make," I told her that night in our dorm room.

Laura turned from the homework she was working on at her desk. "Spill."

It was easier to tell Laura about what happened in the hospital after I'd already confessed to Kellan. Laura didn't interrupt, either. She just sat quietly and listened while I told her about the girls in the hospital and the angel tree they'd made.

"I took Kellan to see the tree, but he flipped," I said. I didn't tell Laura about the story Kellan told me—how he'd been beat up when he was a kid because of his wings—

since I felt like that was his story to share. It wouldn't be fair of me to tell her.

Laura sighed. "Kellan has a point, Cora."

My stomach sank. I knew she didn't agree with me, but I was hoping now that I told her about the girls she might take my side.

I dropped my head in disappointment. "Yeah, everyone seems to be making the same point."

"Then why do you keep pushing it?" she asked. She wasn't being mean. She was honestly curious.

"I don't know," I admitted. "Maybe I'm sick of hiding."

"Me too, Cora, but that doesn't give us the right to expose ourselves," she said gently.

"I know, but it's more than that," I said. "When I flew out of that burning building and showed the world my wings, it was... freeing. We talk about fear all the time. People think if humans knew about us, they'd be afraid. But maybe *we're* the ones who are afraid, Laura."

"We are," she stated. "Everyone's afraid of the unknown, Cora. And we don't know what might happen if everyone knew we existed."

"Exactly," I said. "All I'm saying is it might end up being good."

"Things are fine now, though," Laura insisted. "Why would we want to change things?"

"Because they're *not* fine," I pressed. "Look at what those assholes did to my mom."

Laura's face fell, but she didn't rush to agree with me. Instead, she said, "I think you need to get your mind off this for a while. What do you say we go down to the rec room and play a round of pool?"

I groaned. "I suck at pool. We could go to the Activities Center and fly around."

"Sure," Laura said. "*After* you beat me at pool."

She hopped up from her desk and started pulling on a pair of bright blue heels.

"Fine," I reluctantly agreed.

I pulled on my tennis shoes, and Laura and I headed downstairs to the rec room. When we got there, though, the doors were packed. Inside, we could hear the sound of screaming voices.

"I'm sorry!" a girl squeaked. I recognized the voice as Celina's.

"Sorry!?" Kellan snapped. "Sorry doesn't begin to cover this, Celina."

The sound of Celina's sobs traveled through the open doorway, but I couldn't see inside. Laura and I stepped closer to try to get a good look, but there was a guy blocking our way.

"What's going on?" I asked without really looking at him.

"Sounds like Celina—"

The voice stopped dead when he turned to look at me. My heart stalled in my chest as I looked into dark brown eyes.

Drew.

My high-school boyfriend. The guy I lost my virginity to—who'd dumped me the second we screwed. So far I'd done a pretty good job of avoiding him on campus.

Drew shifted his weight between his feet, like he was uncomfortable around me. Good. He should be after what he did.

He cleared his throat. "Celina cheated on Kellan with Rhys. He just found out."

My stomach dropped to the floor.

"What!?" I shouted so loud that a couple people turned to look at me. Inside, the fight was still going on.

Laura and I exchanged a wide-eyed look.

"Stay away from her!" a deep voice boomed across the rec room.

Rhys. Oh, shit. This couldn't end well.

"I didn't—" Kellan started, but Rhys cut him off.

"You want to go, man? Let's take this outside."

I elbowed my way through the crowd to get to Kellan.

People must've recognized me as his partner, because they made way for me. When I finally broke through the crowd of onlookers, Kellan was backing away from Rhys and Celina. Travis and Caleb stood behind Kellan with their palms held up, like they were ready to conjure essence at a moment's notice. Celina cowered behind Rhys, crying like *she* was the victim. My hands curled into fists, and I wanted nothing more than to throw a fireball at her head.

Kellan shot a scathing look at Celina and scoffed. "Forget it. She's not worth the fight."

Celina's mouth dropped open, but Kellan didn't see it. He whirled around—and slammed straight into me. He stumbled back a step and stared down at me. His eyebrows knitted tightly, and a muscle in his jaw popped. He looked so hurt.

"Kellan," I whispered.

He shook his head at me, like he couldn't bear to talk about it. Then he stepped around me and pushed through the crowd.

"That's right!" Rhys shouted after him. "You better run!"

Behind him, Celina's eyes were filled with tears. She shot daggers my way, then turned to the rest of the crowd. "What are you all still doing here?" she shouted. "The show's over."

Nobody moved, but a few people in the back began whispering.

Rhys took a step forward, his muscled hands flexing at his side. He used his most intimidating voice. "She said the show's over."

The crowd started to disperse. I had a clear shot at the door again, so I started for it.

Laura caught me at the entrance and pointed down the hall. "Kellan went that way."

"Thanks." I hurried off in the direction she pointed.

"So, you caught the end of it?" Travis asked Laura as I was leaving.

"Yeah," she said. "Crazy, right?"

The rest of their conversation faded as I turned the corner. I caught sight of Kellan's blond hair disappear through a door at the end of the hall, and I quickened my pace. I pushed through the door and entered the stairwell. There, I found Kellan sitting on the steps with his head in his hands.

He sighed as he stared down at my shoes, but he didn't move. "What do you want, Cora?"

I lowered myself onto the step beside him. "I'm sorry about what happened."

Kellan gritted his teeth. "What happened with Celina is none of your business."

"But we're partners," I stated. "I'm not going to let you deal with this on your own."

Kellan scoffed and finally lifted his head. I expected his expression to be knitted in anger, but instead, it was full of defeat. Celina had played with his emotions for so long. Last semester, she did all she could to play hard to get. Now she was cheating on him with her partner. It was clear Kellan was exhausted playing this game with her.

"I'm a man," Kellan pointed out. "We're supposed to deal with stuff on our own."

"Well, I'm a girl," I replied. "And we never let our friends deal with a breakup alone."

Kellan let out a puff of air. "Is that what I am? Your friend?"

"Yes," I said. "Haven't we already established that?"

He shrugged. "I just thought after the fight we had earlier, we were back to hating each other."

I shook my head as I stared into his ocean-blue eyes. God, I could get lost in them. My pulse spiked, but the breath in my chest settled as we stared at each other. All I wanted to do was reach over and touch him, to let him know everything was going to be okay. But I resisted.

"I can't stay mad at my partner when we have work to

do," I told him. "We'll make up, but we have to get through this thing with Celina first."

Kellan turned his gaze away from me and stared out the door that went outside. "I don't want to talk about it, Cora."

"Okay," I said gently, but I didn't move. I just sat there in silence.

After a few beats, he added, "To be honest, I kind of want to be alone right now."

His tone was gentle, but my heart broke a little when he said he didn't want me there. And yet I knew that little pang I felt in my chest was nothing compared to what Kellan was feeling now. Screw Celina for doing this to him!

"Okay," I agreed, standing. "But I won't stand around and do nothing about this."

I started for the door that led back into the hall.

"Cora," Kellan groaned.

I didn't stick around to listen to what he had to say. I was still fuming over what Celina had done to him. I flung the door open and stomped down the hall in the direction of the rec room. A few people were standing in the hall, including my group of friends. Travis, Caleb, and Laura were explaining in hushed whispers to Shaylene about what had happened. Travis's eyes flickered upward, and he noticed the determined look on my face.

"Oh, shit," he mumbled. "Cora!"

Travis rushed away from the group and toward me, but I ignored him.

The rec room had completely cleared out, except for Rhys and Celina. They were having a heated conversation but stopped dead in their tracks when I stomped into the room.

Celina's gaze met mine, and she eyed me up and down with disgust. "Look, whatever Kellan told you, I'm sure—"

I walked right past Rhys and shoved Celina in the chest, cutting her off. "You bitch!" I screamed.

A heavy hand landed on my shoulder, but I spun around and slapped Rhys's arm away. A fireball formed in my palm, and I aimed it at the Aedes asshole. "Touch me again, and I'll burn your cheating dick off."

"Not if I burn yours first!" Celina growled from behind me.

I turned to her to see she had a fireball of her own in her hand. She held it up threateningly at me. "Don't fucking mess with Rhys."

"Me?" I balked. "*You're* the one who messed with Kellan."

I noticed my friends in the doorway, but I shot them a look to tell them I had it handled. Laura held Travis back.

"This is none of your business, Cora," Celina spat.

"When it involves my partner, it is!" I shouted.

"Lay off her!" Rhys growled.

He reached for my arm, but I pulled my fire power to the surface, and he jumped back as my skin burned him. He screamed and looked down to his red palm, then turned his angry gaze on me. Rhys lifted his good hand, and black Aedes essence formed inside it. He was a second away from slamming the sphere down on my face to knock me out when four figures jumped in front of him—Travis, Laura, Caleb, and

Shaylene. Two of them raised white Davina essence, while another aimed dark Aedes essence at him. Laura held up Aedes essence in one hand and Davina essence in the other.

She glared at Rhys. "You want to hurt her? You'll have to go through us to do it."

"You think I won't do that?" Rhys threatened her.

Travis stepped forward. He matched Rhys's height, but Rhys had at least twice the muscle mass. And still, Travis didn't show one ounce of fear. "Try it," he sneered. "I dare you."

Rhys curled his upper lip back and stared at Travis several moments longer before backing down.

I turned toward Celina again. She had a hard look on her face, but I could see her quaking in her shoes. "For someone who wanted Kellan to stay at the academy so badly, you really didn't do much yourself to keep him around. Kellan loved you, Celina. And you did nothing but hurt him. I hope you're proud of yourself."

Celina narrowed her eyes at me. "What do you know, Cora? Except how to be annoying."

"I know how to treat people right," I snapped back.

"Well, you clearly don't know how to shut up," she growled. "Kellan was always mine, Cora. Believe me, he'll come crawling back."

"After what you did to him?" I asked. "What makes you so sure?"

"Because Kellan *always* comes back to me," she stated confidently, crossing her arms. "Besides, if you think he's going to go crying to you just because you're his partner, you better think again. Kellan would rather cut his own wings off than date you."

I totally lost it. Joking about cutting your wings off was unacceptable. To even suggest Kellan would do that to himself was lower than low.

I couldn't listen to her talk anymore. I lifted my palm and formed a white ball of essence inside of it. I was about to throw it straight into her face, but I didn't get a chance before she thrust her hands out and essence shot straight at me.

I ducked, and the essence soared over my head. Travis leapt out of the way, and the essence slammed straight into Rhys's chest. His eyes rolled back in his skull as he was stunned, and his huge body crumbled to the ground.

Celina's eyes went big, and her lips curled into a sneer. She readied her hands to throw another ball of essence at me, but another hand shot out of nowhere and caught her wrist.

The essence in my hand fizzled out as Kellan stepped in front of me. "Don't talk to Cora like that, Celina," he demanded as he dropped her wrists.

She stared at Kellan wide-eyed, like she couldn't believe he was standing up for me. "Why not? You hate her, too."

Kellan chuckled lightly, but it sounded stilted and forced. "Not as much as I hate you. Believe me, I won't be crawling back this time. I hope you and Rhys are fucking happy."

And then Kellan whirled around and strolled out of the room. My friends and I exchanged a quick glance of shock, but I was the fastest to recover. I hurried out into the hall after him.

"Kellan!" I called.

He was already standing next to the elevator and pushing the button. He pressed his hand to his temple when he saw me coming, like the stress was too much right now.

"Kellan, I'm sorry," I said as I came to a stop beside him. "I hope I didn't make it worse."

"No," he sighed. "It was already bad enough."

The elevator doors opened, and Kellan stepped inside. I hesitated for a moment, but he stepped to the side, like he was waiting for me to join him. I stepped inside the elevator, and Kellan pressed the button for his floor.

Once the elevator started moving, a silent beat passed before Kellan said, "Thanks for what you did, Cora."

"What do you mean?" I asked. "I didn't do anything."

"You did," he replied. "You stood up for me."

I shrugged. "Well, yeah. That's what partners do."

Or girls who are hopelessly in love with you. Whichever.

The elevator doors opened, and we both stepped off. This wasn't my floor, but I found myself following him back to his dorm room anyway.

Kellan shoved his hands into his pockets. "This was different, Cora. You didn't stand up for me because you're my partner. You stood up for me because..."

"Because we're friends?" I filled in for him when he trailed off.

"Yeah," he breathed. "Because we're friends."

Kellan stopped at his door, but he didn't go inside right

away. He just stood there awkwardly, like there was more he wanted to say.

He cleared his throat. "Anyway… thanks, Cora."

And then the strangest thing happened. Kellan reached out and pulled me into a hug. My heart jumped as his warmth surrounded me. A fresh linen scent filled my nose. I was surprised at first, but I found myself relaxing into the hug. I hadn't felt this relaxed in… well, forever.

Being in Kellan's arms was indescribable. I'd dreamt about this moment for weeks—what it'd feel like to do this and more to him. But I didn't ever dream it would feel so… right. I thought I'd be scared. And part of me was. But a larger part of me didn't know why, because being in his arms felt perfect, like I was right where I was meant to be.

As I wrapped my arms around him to hug him back, Kellan's arms pulled even tighter around me. Then he ducked down, and I thought my heart was about to give out. His lips connected with my forehead. A warm sensation tingled down my body and back up again, making my heart rate spike.

Kellan instantly dropped me, like he was just as surprised as I was. I stepped away and cleared my throat, because even though I was sure the hug was meant to happen, I didn't think he'd intended to kiss me.

Sure, it wasn't a *real* kiss. It wasn't even on the lips. But it was a kiss nonetheless, and even as partners we weren't supposed to get *that* close.

"I should probably, um…" I started.

"Yeah, me too." Kellan reached for his door handle. "See you later, Cora."

"Bye."

Kellan rushed into his room so quickly, you'd think there was an ax murderer coming down the hall or something. I just stood there in shock for several moments longer, wondering where the affection had come from.

It was the heat of the moment, I told myself. But a part of me wasn't sure if that was true... or if there was something more to it.

I didn't see Kellan until our Art of Healing II lecture the next week. He glanced at me from across the room, but I couldn't read his expression. I, on the other hand, blushed red like a freaking tomato. The guy did things to me that no one else could. I didn't get it.

I sat in my usual spot in the lecture hall beside Laura and Shaylene. I sank in my seat a little, trying to hide behind the trio of girls who sat in front of me. Sarah was showing Avery and Lisa a video on her phone. They had their heads close together, so it was easy to hide behind them.

Laura eyed me, and her lips curled into a teasing smirk.

"*Someone's* embarrassed," she sang lowly so only Shaylene and I could hear.

Shaylene followed my gaze, and her eyes landed on Kellan. She sat up straighter in her chair, her black wings brushing up against the table behind us. "Wait. Did something happen?"

I sighed. "No, nothing happened."

Laura leaned over and lowered her voice. "He kissed her."

"What!?" Shaylene balked. "Cora, why didn't you tell me."

"It wasn't a *real* kiss," I insisted. "We just hugged, and he kind of... kissed me on the forehead."

"That means something," Shaylene said.

"That's what I told her," Laura agreed.

"No, you guys," I groaned. "It's nothing. It was just a friendly thing between two partners. It meant nothing."

Shaylene scoffed and turned to face the front of the room. "Okay. If you say so."

Professor Kovski entered the room, and the chatter slowly died. She pulled up her lecture notes on the projector and dove right in. "Welcome, class. Last week I hinted that we'd be studying a very important concept today that you wouldn't want to miss."

She pressed a button on her remote, and the word *Channeling* came up on the screen. My spine straightened as I opened my laptop to take notes. I'd heard so much about channeling but didn't really know how it worked. I was really excited to learn.

"Channeling is an advanced type of healing power," Professor Kovski continued. "It's not something we practice in this class, but it's an important topic to cover, especially for those students who are accepted into our upper-level programs. So, what exactly *is* channeling?"

Professor Kovski changed the slide again, and a drawing appeared. It showed a patient lying on a bed with a glowing ball of essence hovering above them. "Channeling is a technique where a Davina transfers—or *channels*—their essence into another being's body. It intertwines with their life force and places them in a suspended state. Think of it as a medically-induced coma. It buys time in serious cases to administer blood transfusions or diagnose more serious issues."

I was so entranced by the concept that I found myself leaning forward over my table.

Professor Kovski pressed another button on her remote, and the drawing began to animate. It showed the essence lowering into the patient's mouth and then spreading throughout their body. "Once the essence enters a patients' body, it can stay there for up to twenty-four hours without causing damage. Once it's job is complete, the essence must be removed."

The animation changed to show the essence drawing out of the patient's body and forming into the glowing white ball again.

"As you can imagine, this technique is much different than the healing we've been practicing over the last two semesters," Professor Kovski said. "It requires a great deal of care and intent. I expect a two-page paper on this concept from each of you by the end of the week."

"That was a cool lecture," Laura said as we left the lecture hall.

Shaylene brushed out her dark hair with her fingers. "Agreed. Anyone want to get some grub?"

I shrugged. "I could eat."

We left the Science Building—and stopped in our tracks. A shadow passed above us, and the three of us looked up to see someone with black wings flying overhead. They were flying high, way higher than the walls of campus, which was totally off-limits in case someone outside saw.

I shaded my eyes to get a better look. "What is he—oh my God!"

As I watched the Aedes fly above us, I realized his flight trajectory was off, and he was teetering in the sky. Whoever it was took a nose-dive, and my stomach dropped as he tumbled toward the ground.

Laura, Shaylene, and I raced in the direction of the Aedes, but before we could get there, another flash of black wings streaked past us. I gasped when I saw it was Kellan. The first Aedes was about to plummet into a pile of melting snow when Kellan swooped in and caught him by the shoulders at the last second. He slowly lowered him to the ground as we raced over.

"Oh God!" Laura's hands slapped over her mouth. "What happened?"

We stopped beside the two of them, who were slumped on the slushy ground. My guts twisted when I saw the state the Aedes guy was in. He was shirtless and had bruises all over his torso. Huge chunks of feathers were missing from his wings, and his eyes rolled back into his skull. With his ruffled hair and a swollen black eye, it took me a second to realize that I recognized him.

It was Kumar, the fourth-year Aedes who'd led my orientation group my first day at the academy.

"Kumar!" Kellan slapped his face a little to get him to wake up.

Kumar's eyelids fluttered, but he didn't completely come to.

"What happened?" I heard Travis ask from behind me.

By now, a huge group had formed, mostly the people who had been leaving our Art of Healing II lecture when Kumar flew overhead.

I immediately jumped into emergency mode. I turned to see Travis and Caleb looking shell-shocked but eager to help. "Travis and Caleb, go get Chancellor Harris. Shaylene and Laura, we need Professor Kovski out here right away."

"Got it!" Travis gave me a salute, and the four of them ran off.

Sarah, one of the girls who sat in front of me in class, looked at me like she wanted to help.

"Sarah, go tell the nurses," I instructed.

"On it," she said, grabbing her two friends and whirling around. The three of them rushed toward the health services center.

I leaned down to Kumar's level and took his hand in mine. He squeezed it ever so slightly, so I knew he was still conscious, but barely.

"Kumar, take my essence," I told him.

He groaned a little, but his head lolled to the side like he didn't hear me.

"Kumar," I stated firmly. "You're badly hurt. Essence will help you heal. Take mine."

A familiar electric sizzle passed over my hand as he started drawing my essence into himself. It wasn't a lot, but it lifted his energy enough that his eyes opened.

"Chancellor Harris," Kumar groaned. "I need to talk to Chancellor Harris."

"She's coming," Kellan stated. "You just lie back and relax, buddy."

Kellan stripped off his jacket and laid it over Kumar. I shifted to cradle Kumar's head in my lap. He shivered from the cold, but he relaxed his head.

"They've got Annie," Kumar groaned.

"Annie?" I asked.

Kumar inhaled a sharp breath and stilled. "My sister."

I gasped. *Annie.* We'd played aerial soccer with her last semester.

"Who has her?" Kellan demanded.

"I-I don't know," Kumar admitted. "The Infantry, I think."

My hands curled into fists. "Colt has your sister?"

"I don't know," Kumar said through clenched teeth. "I didn't see their faces. They jumped us downtown. They sent me back to give Chancellor Harris a message."

"What message?" a stern female voice demanded.

My gaze snapped upward, and I saw Chancellor Harris pushing through the crowd. She wore a light t-shirt, like she'd rushed out of her office without her coat. Travis and Caleb looked worried behind her.

"Everyone out of the way!" Professor Kovski shouted.

She ran in from the other side of the crowd, and people parted to let her through.

Professor Kovski knelt down at Kumar's side and placed her hands over his stomach. She closed her eyes. I could tell by the knitted concentration in her face that she was using her essence to diagnose his injuries.

A few moments later, Professor Kovski opened her eyes and announced, "He's suffering from intense internal bleeding. We need to get him to the health services center."

Chancellor Harris turned to the crowd. "Everyone return to your dorms or classes immediately."

The crowd began to disperse, all except me and Kellan, since Kumar was still holding on to us. Our friends shot us a look before they left, as if to say they'd be waiting for us whenever we were ready. I nodded back to let them know we'd see them soon.

Professor Kovski stood and pulled her phone to her ear, while Chancellor Harris knelt in the snow beside Kumar.

"Kumar," she said softly. "What's the message?"

Kumar swallowed and licked his lips. "They want to talk to you, Chancellor. If you don't, they're going to kill Annie."

13

I was reeling from what happened in the courtyard with Kumar as I walked beside Kellan back to our dorm. Professor Sanders had arrived shortly after with a stretcher, and they took him away to be healed, while Kellan and I were dismissed. Everything happened so fast, and we were still trying to process what Kumar had told us.

"This is bad, Kellan," I said. "Really bad."

He swallowed. "I know."

I had so many questions, I didn't even know where to start. How did they know Kumar and Annie were supernatural? Had they followed them from campus? Did they attack Kumar in the middle of downtown during daylight hours, or did they take him somewhere else? What had they done to Annie, and how badly was she hurt? Was it safe to leave campus?

And most importantly, was it safe to stay?

I wasn't sure how long it would take to get answers.

"I'm scared," I admitted.

Kellan stopped just before the front doors of our dorm. He grabbed me by the shoulders and turned me to face him. "Nothing's going to happen to you, Cora. I won't let it."

My heart fluttered in my chest. I spoke in a small voice. "I'm not scared for me, Kellan. I'm scared for everyone else. I don't want anyone else getting hurt."

Kellan stared deep into my eyes. When he spoke, it was like a binding promise he'd never dare to break. "We're not going to let that happen, Cora. Come on."

He cocked his head toward the door. When we stepped inside, we found our friends sitting in the main study area by the front desk. Caleb sat on the couch and had his arm around Shaylene. Laura fidgeted in her chair, and Travis paced back and forth.

Travis stopped in his tracks when he saw us. "Did you learn what happened?"

Kellan shook his head. "All we know is someone jumped them downtown and hurt them. They're threatening to kill Annie if Chancellor Harris doesn't talk to them."

Laura's hands shot over her mouth. "Oh, God. She's going to talk to them, right?"

"She has to," I stated firmly. There was no alternative.

Laura's shoulders shook. "I can't believe this is happening."

Caleb shook his head, but his eyes weren't really focused on anything. "It's crazy. Annie's one of our own. We're in classes together."

"Yeah, she sits by us in our earth element class," Travis said. "She wasn't there today, but I never imagined it was… this."

"No one could've known this was going to happen to her," I stated.

"No," Kellan agreed, "but we have to do something about it."

"Do *what*?" I asked. "Go after Colt? We don't even know if it was him."

Kellan crossed his arms. "You don't know he burnt down your mom's restaurant, either, but you seem pretty adamant it was him. Don't you want to get back at him?"

"Of course I do," I snapped. "But we're not the Alliance."

Kellan's features hardened. "No, but they haven't dealt with Colt yet. *Someone* has to do something."

Laura's eyes lit up in interest. "What are you suggesting?"

Kellan raked his hands through his blond hair. "I don't know yet. A sort of security team, maybe?"

"I'm in!" Travis raised his hand before hearing any more.

"Me, too," Caleb agreed.

I crossed my arms. "And me."

"Wait." Shaylene shot to her feet. "You guys aren't suggesting like a vigilante group, are you?"

Kellan raised an eyebrow at her. "And if we are?"

"Violence isn't going to solve violence," she pointed out.

The room went silent, and I held my breath. After what Colt did to my mom, I wanted nothing more than to stab my Davina Blade into his chest. But Shaylene's words made me pause. I could do anything I wanted to Colt, but who's to say someone bigger and badder wouldn't rise up to get revenge on *us*? She had a point.

Travis cracked his knuckles. "Violence will solve something, I'm sure."

"Maybe our group could be about facilitating peace," I suggested.

Kellan sighed, like he was sick of me suggesting this. "This again, Cora?"

I turned on him, my nostrils flaring. *I* was sick of him shooting me down every time the topic came up. "My parents did it," I snapped. "Or maybe you forgot that thirty years ago, you and I would be trying to kill each other."

Kellan pressed his lips together, like he was trying hard not to shoot back an insult. His ever-changing mood left me in a constant state of whiplash.

"Either way," Kellan said coolly, "I can't sit around doing nothing. Annie's out there, possibly being tortured."

"I agree," I said, "but do you have any ideas on what we can do?"

"We're sitting ducks until we know more," Kellan said. "I'll talk to Kumar as soon as he's stable."

"Okay," I agreed. "But Kellan…"

Kellan stared down at me. Though he had a look of determination painted on his face, I saw the ache beneath it. None of us knew Annie well, but she was one of us. I could tell Kellan was taking it particularly hard because of what happened to him when he was a kid.

I took a long breath. "Whatever we do, we do it together."

It was late by the time the health services center returned Kellan's call and said he could come and visit Kumar. While Kellan went to talk to him, I headed to Chancellor Harris's office.

I walked through the darkness with my hands shoved in my pockets for warmth. I glanced around campus. It was quiet and a little eerie. I knew the Infantry couldn't get inside the walls. After what happened today, I was sure the academy had increased security. But still, I had images of the Infantry crawling over the walls and swarming the school to torture us all.

But nothing happened. I reached the Academy Building in one piece and walked upstairs to Chancellor Harris's office. Her receptionist wasn't at her desk, so I walked past it and knocked on the double doors. I didn't know what I was expecting, but no answer came. Of course she wasn't here. She was obviously dealing with the shit the Infantry was stirring up.

And then came the sound of heels clicking against the tile. I turned around to see Chancellor Harris rushing down the hall. When her eyes caught mine, she looked surprised.

"Cora, can I help you?" She spoke quickly, like she was in a rush.

"We want to help, Chancellor," I said.

She paused for a moment, then reached for her door. "Inside, Cora."

She rushed me into her office. I didn't even sit before I started talking. "Chancellor Harris, what's going on?"

She paced across the room and stood at the window. "It's the Infantry, Cora."

Surprise, surprise.

"They're holding a student hostage," she told me solemnly.

"What do they want?" I asked.

She pressed her lips together firmly and gazed out over campus. "They're making demands we simply can't meet."

My stomach plummeted to my toes. "Wait, so you can't save Annie?"

Her gaze snapped to mine. "We will. I assure you of that. But… it's complicated."

"What sort of demands are they making?" I questioned.

Chancellor Harris hesitated, as if unsure whether or not to tell me the truth. Finally, she said, "They want to expose the school."

"I thought you wanted us to expose ourselves," I mentioned.

She shook her head. "Not like this, Cora. Not on their terms. They intent to incite a panic. It could put the entire student body in jeopardy—not just Annie."

"So, how can we help?" I asked desperately. I'd do anything to protect my fellow students.

Chancellor Harris sat in her chair, looking defeated. "We need to change their minds."

I gaped at her. "How do we do that?"

She shook her head. "I don't know yet, Cora. But I have a call I have to make. I appreciate your eagerness to help, but I'm afraid there's just not much you can do right now."

"Thank you," I said. I knew whatever call she had to make was important, so I left the room quickly.

I was walking back to my dorm when I caught sight of Laura and Shaylene walking near the Winged Fountain. They'd left to get takeout from the dining hall before I'd gone to meet Chancellor Harris, but they had no food in their hands.

They both walked at a quick pace and looked around frantically. I could hear their voices traveling over the courtyard, but I couldn't make out what they were saying. The street lamps above them illuminated their faces, and I instantly became worried when I saw the expression of distress they shared. Their eyes landed on me, and they rushed over.

"Thank God," Laura said breathlessly. "We thought you guys had left without us."

"Left where?" I asked.

Shaylene pulled her coat tighter around her. "We don't know. The guys sent us to grab food, but when we got back, everyone was gone."

My body tensed. "Everyone? I know Kellan went to talk to Kumar."

"Well, Travis and Caleb disappeared," Laura stated.

"You don't think they're in trouble, do you?" I asked.

Laura crossed her arms. "Travis? In trouble? He hears the word danger, and he goes running after it."

"You don't think—?" I started, but Laura nodded, cutting me off. "You think they went after Annie?"

Laura's lips tightened. "Well, if Kellan found out where she was, what's to stop them?"

My hands tightened into fists. "We have to go help them! They could get themselves killed."

"Exactly," Shaylene said. "Except we don't know where they went."

I pulled my phone out of my pocket and punched the screen.

Where are you!? I texted Kellan.

No response.

I huffed. "I bet they did this on purpose."

"Left us girls behind?" Shaylene asked, sounding less than pleased.

"Yes," I said. "We talked about doing this peacefully. They don't want our help."

Shaylene's features darkened. "Caleb's going to get an earful from me tonight. Jerk."

A silent beat passed as we all considered what to do next.

"We have to go talk to Kumar," I finally said. "If he told Kellan where Annie is, he can tell us. We can go after them and help."

"Or get everyone in deeper trouble," Laura pointed out.

"Well, I can't just sit around," I said.

I wasn't taking no for an answer. Laura finally caved, and the three of us walked to the health services center. But when we got there, the receptionist told us that visiting hours were over. She wouldn't let us through to Kumar, no matter how much we argued.

There was nothing we could do but wait for them. We

returned to the Winged Fountain, since it gave the widest view of campus. We sat on the edge and shivered in the cold, but the three of us were determined to remain put until the guys returned.

It must've been an hour before we spotted the shadows in the sky. They were hard to see in the darkness, but I caught sight of dark wings against the backdrop of the moon.

The three of us shot to our feet as a group of guys swooped down onto campus and landed near the health services center. It wasn't just Kellan, Caleb, and Travis, either. There were at least a dozen other guys behind them. Most of them rushed inside, but three others hung back.

My friends and I ran over to them. They were all talking over each other and sounded distressed. Travis was shirtless with his wings out, and he paced back and forth with his hands fisted at his sides. Caleb and a guy I'd only met once, Tucker, were trying to calm him down.

"We should've burned that place to the ground!" Travis growled.

"Oh my God, you guys!" I cried as I sprinted over. "What happened?"

"Travis!" Laura gasped. "Are you okay?"

She reached up to the side of his face, which was swollen and bruised. He wrapped her in a hug. "Don't worry, babe. I'm Davina. I'll heal fast."

I looked around for Kellan, but I didn't see him. My breath stalled in my chest.

Caleb must've noticed, because he grabbed my arm. "He's fine, Cora. He's inside."

My stomach twisted into knots when he said Kellan was in the health services center. Had something bad happened to him?

I didn't ask. I just ran into the building and down the hall. When I got inside the doors to the health center, my heart lurched. Voices filled the entrance as nurses yelled instructions back and forth. Kellan was standing in front of the reception desk and placing a petite, unconscious girl onto a gurney the nurses had pulled out for her.

Annie.

She looked really pale and had gashes running up and down her arms. Her black wings were out and were twisted at odd angles.

Two other guys were being guided onto gurneys. One was unconscious and being carried by two other guys, and another was clutching his stomach and groaning as he lay down. I recognized the guys. The one clutching his stomach was Jett, a guy I'd barely met before but saw at a party once. Then there was Miles, a tall guy from my fire-fighting classes, and Everett, a Water Davina, carrying the unconscious guy together.

I didn't see who it was at first, until his head lolled to the side. I gasped when I caught sight of his face. It was Drew, my ex-boyfriend. I barely had a second to process it before he and Annie were being wheeled down the hall.

Kellan himself was shirtless, with his black wings on display. He was bleeding from a large wound on his shoulder. It looked like a bullet wound. My throat closed up as I took in his injuries. Just the thought of him being hurt worried me to my very core.

"Kellan!" I cried as I rushed over to him.

He let out a breath. "Spare me the lecture, Cora. I did what I had to do."

"You're shot!" I yelled.

"Sir," a nurse said to Kellan. "Sir, you're going to have to come with me."

"No," he snapped at her, but he quickly softened his tone. "Take care of the others first."

Her lips tightened, but they were obviously short-staffed at this time of night, so she didn't argue. "I'll get you some gauze for that, and we'll patch you up shortly."

Kellan turned back to me.

I had half a mind not to punch him in his injured shoulder. "You jerk! I thought we agreed that whatever happened, we'd do it together."

He gazed down at me with a soft expression. I didn't know if it was because he was kind of out of it from blood loss or if he was happy to see me. "I never agreed to that, Cora. But I am truly sorry about lying to you. I just knew you'd never agree to it."

He shifted his weight between his feet and glanced around the room.

I took Kellan's face in my hands and forced him to look me in the eye. I was so pissed at him right now, but I couldn't bring myself to fight when he was hurt like this. "What matters is everyone made it out, right?"

Kellan nodded as the nurse handed him the gauze. "Yeah, we all made it out. But Miles and Annie are hurt real bad. I didn't know they'd have guns."

The nurse turned to me. "You keep an eye on him, and if anything happens, you come and get me."

"Got it," I said.

The nurse rushed off after the others whose injuries were more life-threatening.

Kellan pressed the gauze to his wound and winced. He looked at me, but he could hardly focus.

"You need to sit." I grabbed his good arm and guided him over to the waiting area.

Kellan breathed a sigh of relief once he sat down.

"I can heal this if you let me," I offered. "As long as the bullet's not still in there."

He shook his head. "I got it out."

"Okay," I said gently, "but I'm going to have to double check. Do you trust me to diagnose it?"

Kellan nodded.

"I'm going to need your help," I reminded him.

Kellan grabbed my arm with his good hand and squeezed so tightly that I squeaked a little. He closed his eyes and gritted his teeth.

"Kellan, stay with me," I demanded. "We've got this."

I pulled the gauze away to look at the injury, but it was still oozing blood. I placed my hand over the wound and pushed my essence into it to explored his injuries. I could feel the warmth of his pain. There was a lot of tissue damage and grime shoved into the wound, but his immune system would take care of the bacteria once I healed it.

"It feels like all the bullet fragments are out," I said. "You ready?"

Kellan nodded, then started opening my essence channel. I guided warm, fuzzy essence into his wound, and my hand began to glow. He sighed in relief, and I knew his pain was melting away. It was a deep wound, so it took a while to heal, but it was simple, so I was able to sterilize it and close it up easily with my magic.

When I drew away, his shoulder looked as if he'd never been shot in the first place. I wiped the blood away with the gauze. "How does that feel?"

Kellan took my wrist, stopping me from wiping his shoulder. I glanced up to him, and he was starting at me in this intense way—almost like he wanted to kiss me. My breath stalled in my chest, but my heart sped up. Even though I was mad at him for going after Annie without me, I couldn't help but feel like I was melting in his presence.

"A little sore yet," he admitted softly without taking his eyes off me. "But I'll be fine now... Thanks to you."

Our eyes locked for several more seconds. His gaze flickered to my lips, and I felt a surge of excitement rush through my belly. Then another tingling rushed through me. My essence channel shot open, and power whipped through me, making my whole body come alive with an electric charge.

Kellan jerked away and dropped my arm. "Sorry. I didn't mean to do that. I just... needed the power-up."

He didn't sound convincing, though I didn't know why else he would take my essence like that.

"It's okay," I assured him. "You can take as much as you need. You've been through a lot tonight."

Then, without giving myself a chance to second guess it, I took his arm and put it over my shoulder, and I laid my head on his shoulder. It wasn't meant as a romantic gesture, just a way for us to keep in contact so he could channel my essence and heal faster. But I'd never felt so comfortable and at ease in someone else's arms. He didn't pull away, either.

Kellan relaxed. "Thanks, Cora."

After a few moments of silence, I said, "So, are you going to tell me what happened?"

"Do you really want to know?" he asked.

"Yes, I really want to know," I stated. "Why'd you ditch me? We're partners. We're supposed to do this kind of thing together."

He shrugged. "Because you'd never have let me go through with it. When Kumar told me where they were keeping Annie, I just… I lost it. When I got back to the dorms to get Travis and Caleb, they already had a group of guys together who wanted to help. And so…"

"You went after her," I finished for him.

He sighed. "It was risky, I know. It goes against every-thing we've been taught at the academy. But we got her."

"So, where *were* they keeping her?" I asked.

"She was at this abandoned warehouse on the other side of the city," Kellan said.

"And it was the Infantry?" I questioned. "You saw them?"

Kellan hesitated a moment. "Well, sort of. As soon as we got in, they put on ski masks and started shooting at us. We didn't see their faces."

I bit my lower lip. We now had two major crimes that I was sure connected in some way—the arson at my mom's restaurant and Annie's kidnapping. But we still had no proof who'd done it.

"Cora, it's them," he stated confidently.

"It's Colt?" I asked. I already knew it was him, but having the confirmation would be freeing. The last thing I needed was to be focusing on Colt when there was some other asshole out there hurting my people.

Kellan nodded. "I didn't see him, but I heard their leader shouting orders. It sounded just like him."

"I believe you, Kellan," I said. "But we have to be very careful going forward. I want to get back at him as much as you do, but hurting him is only going to make us bigger targets. I can't risk them going after my family again."

"You're right."

I was shocked to hear him say it. "You agree with me?"

His shoulders fell. "After tonight, we've all become targets. I've dragged other people into this, and they got hurt."

I sniffled. "Kellan, what are we going to do?"

"Excuse me?" A nurse walked into the waiting room and looked to us. "Are you Cora?"

I sat up straight. The air felt cold between Kellan and me. "I am."

She cleared her throat. "Drew Randall is asking for you. Would you like to see him?"

Drew was asking for *me*? Shit. It must've been really bad if my ex wanted to talk to me.

"Yes," I answered as I shot to my feet. "Yes, I'd like to see him."

I walked into Drew's room on shaky knees. The nurse shut the door behind us to give us privacy. Drew sat on the bed and looked up at me. His face was pale, like he'd lost a lot of blood, but he was alert.

I stopped a few paces from his bed, feeling really awkward being there alone with him. We hadn't really talked in over a year. I had no idea what he could possibly want from me.

"Did the wound heal okay?" I squeaked out.

Drew cleared his throat and nodded. "They healed the wound. My body will take care of any internal injuries within a few days. Perks of being a Davina."

He gave a nervous chuckle, but it sounded stale. He must've felt just as awkward as I did.

I steeled my nerves and looked him straight in the eye. "Why'd you ask me to come in here, Drew?"

He took a deep breath and gestured to the chair beside his bed. "You should probably sit down for this."

My heart pounded as I sat. A long silence stretched between us, until I dared to break it. "What is this about?"

Drew couldn't meet my gaze. "I have a confession to make, Cora. After I was shot tonight, I thought I might not make it. My buddies tried to heal me on location, but we were so rushed and everyone was hyped up on adrenaline… the only thing we could do was come back to school."

I swallowed the lump in my throat. I couldn't imagine what he'd gone through tonight—what any of them had gone through.

Drew continued. "While they were flying me back and I was bleeding out, all these things started to rush through my mind."

He paused for a moment, and I dared to ask, "What kind of things?"

He frowned. "Things I'd done wrong."

He paused for a moment before continuing. "I was really out of it when they brought me back, but I saw you out there by the waiting room. It just made me think of what a jerk I was to you."

My stomach sank at the memories. Drew was the one and only guy I'd gone all the way with—and he dumped me the second he had what he wanted. He didn't even have the decency to do it in person. I had to find out we were breaking up over text.

"I just wanted to apologize, Cora," Drew said softly.

The look in his eyes told me he was being honest. It was hard to wrap my head around after the way he treated me in high school. But it was like there was something different about him now. I didn't know if it was because he'd grown in the year we'd spent apart, or if tonight had changed him.

"Cora?" Drew pressed.

It took me a second to realize I'd been sitting there for several moments without responding. I never thought I'd hear him apologize.

"It's fine, Drew," I found myself saying, though it was hard to get the words out.

"No, it's not, Cora," he insisted. "You're doing that thing again."

"What thing?" I asked.

"That thing you did when we broke up," he said. "You act like everything's fine when it's not. I know you hold the breakup against me."

It was true. I hadn't really ever gotten over it.

I shrugged. "It was a long time ago."

"I know," he said gently. "And it still hurts."

My breath stopped in its tracks. "I guess so," I admitted.

After a beat, Drew spoke again. "I want to join your cause, Cora."

I furrowed my brow. "My cause?"

He nodded. "I know you and Kellan are leading the charge. Whatever we have to do to keep what happened to Annie from happening again, I'm in."

"Even though you were shot?" I balked.

"Yes," he said simply. "But I don't want to ruin anything by causing tension between us. I just hope we can put the past aside and work together."

My chest softened at his offer. "I'd like that, too, Drew."

His eyes brightened. "So, you forgive me?"

I bit my lower lip. Instinct told me to say yes, but I didn't know if that was just because I was feeling sympathetic since he'd been shot. I'd spent so long holding it all against him that it was hard to let that go.

But I knew the future wasn't about me. It was about all of us.

"I'm going to try," I told him.

He breathed a huge sigh of relief, like he'd been carrying around a huge weight. "Thank you, Cora."

15

week passed, and news about Annie and the rescue mission had spread throughout the school. Everywhere we went, people approached Kellan to ask about it. He gave curt answers and seemed annoyed when people commended him for his bravery.

"I didn't do this to be recognized as some sort of hero," he told me in our firefighting class one day. "I did it to save Annie."

"And you *did* save her," I pointed out. "But isn't all this recognition good for you? It could help you get a position on the Alliance like you want."

Kellan thought about it for a moment. "Yeah, I guess you're right. But people seem to keep forgetting that I got people hurt."

"Everyone's healed," I reminded him. "Drew was the worst, and he's out of the hospital."

Kellan raked his fingers through his blond hair. "Yeah,

118

but I just keep thinking of how I'd do it differently. He never would've gotten hurt in the first place."

"You don't know that," I said.

Kellan sighed. "That meeting with Chancellor Harris didn't help how I feel about this, either."

Kellan had already told me about what went down in that meeting. Chancellor Harris and a bunch of faculty came together to reprimand the guys about going off and saving Annie without consulting anyone. They made a big deal out of how even though they were glad Annie was safe, they could've royally screwed things up and gotten her—and themselves—killed.

"Anyway," Kellan said. "Are you coming tonight?"

I furrowed my brow. "Coming where?"

He looked shocked that I didn't know what he was talking about. "To Heaven's Lounge."

"The bar beneath the dining center?" I asked.

He nodded. "Kumar invited us all out as a sort of thank-you."

"I guess I wasn't invited," I said.

Kellan nudged me in the arm. "Well, you can come as my date."

My heart lifted in my chest when he said it, but the look in his eyes told me he didn't mean it in that way.

"Say you'll come," he begged.

A blush rose to my cheeks. "Okay, I'll come."

∽

Kellan came to my dorm room that night, and we walked to Heaven's Lounge together. The place was so packed we could hardly see to the back wall. The lighting was dim to begin with, so that made it even harder to spot our friends. I scanned the room, but I didn't see our friends anywhere near the bar or at the dining tables up front. I spotted Celina, but I was staying the hell away from her. I noticed Kellan's eyes fall on her for a second, but they continued to sweep the room, like he didn't care.

"There they are," Kellan said, eyeing the back corner.

My heart leapt when he took my hand and led me through the crowd. We found our friends seated at a long table that was really four tables pushed together. Travis and Laura sat side-by-side, with his arm draped around her. Caleb and Shaylene were trying to throw peanuts in each other's mouths from across the table. Kumar sat at the head of the table and was chatting with Drew and Miles while he sipped on a beer. Everyone else was here—all the guys Kellan had recruited to help the other night.

When Kumar's eyes landed on Kellan, he jumped to his feet. "Kellan, my man!"

He came over to us and shook Kellan's hand, then pulled him into a one-armed hug. "How've you been, our big hero?"

He clapped him on the shoulder, then turned to the rest of the group. "Everyone, Kellan's here!"

A chorus of *hellos* traveled around the table.

I could tell Kumar was already a little drunk. He turned to Kellan and lowered his voice. "Thanks for saving my sister, man. I owe you big time."

Kellan's eyes roamed the table. "Is she joining us?"

"Nah," Kumar said. "She's staying with our parents for a while. It's safer that way. But she's doing a lot better."

"That's good to hear," Kellan said.

"Hey, why don't you take a seat," Kumar suggested. "Can I get you anything to drink?"

Kellan waved his hand. "Nah, I'm good."

"Pft," Kumar said. "I'll grab you a beer."

"Cora!" Laura called over the loud chatter. "We saved you guys seats!"

Kellan and I sat next to each other in the empty chairs beside Laura and Travis. It was only after I sat that I realized Drew was on my other side.

Great. I was sandwiched between the only two guys I'd ever had feelings for.

Drew noticed me immediately and offered a friendly smile. "Hey, Cora. How are you?"

"Fine," I said.

Kellan heard us talking, and his curiosity piqued. "You two know each other?"

I nodded. "Yeah, we went to high school together. Drew's my…" I trailed off when I realized I was about to say *ex-boyfriend*. Was that the right way to introduce him?

Drew cleared his throat. "We used to go out."

Kellan's face fell. I'd never told him about Drew or anything that happened between us, but he seemed to sense it wasn't good. "Oh," he said flatly.

When Drew turned away to talk to the guy next to him, Kellan leaned into me and lowered his voice. "Do you need to switch seats with me?"

My pulse quickened as his warm breath rushed across the side of my face. "No, I'm fine."

"Here you go." Kumar reached between us and set a beer in front of Kellan. Kellan wasn't twenty-one yet, but I didn't think anyone would notice or check his I.D.

"Thanks," he said, before taking a swig of beer.

"No problem," Kumar replied. "If you need another, you know who to ask."

He winked, then went back to his seat at the head of the table. The guys around him were all laughing and goofing off.

"Hey, Cora," Caleb called. "Open wide."

Before I could respond, he tossed a peanut at my face. It bounced off, and I caught it in my hand.

I laughed and threw it back at him. "Hey! I wasn't ready."

"Try me," Kellan said.

Caleb picked a peanut up from the bowl in front of him and tossed it at Kellan. He caught it in his mouth and ate it.

"Dude, you're a pro," Caleb teased.

Kellan shrugged and reached for a menu. "Or lucky."

Caleb held up a second peanut. "Another?"

"Nah, man," Kellan said. "I'm going to quit while I'm ahead."

"Toss me one." I opened my mouth wide, and it took two more tries before Caleb got one in my mouth.

We hung out for another hour, laughing with our friends and listening to Travis and Caleb tell stories of their parkour adventures, some of which I wasn't sure I bought. Kellan and I split an order of fries.

"Do you need another drink?" he asked, gesturing to my empty soda.

"If you're getting up, sure," I said.

My eyes followed Kellan as he walked up to the bar. Laura noticed me checking out his backside and shot me a knowing smile. I blushed and ducked my head. When my gaze darted back toward Kellan, my stomach dropped.

Kellan walked by a beefy guy and accidentally bumped into him, causing him to spill his drink on himself. When he turned around, I saw that it was Rhys. His lips curled into a sneer, and he puffed out his chest like he was trying to assert his dominance. Kellan took a step back, and the two exchanged a few words I couldn't hear. I was already on my feet, rushing over to him as back-up. Not like Kellan needed it, though.

"No need to get all bent out of shape," Kellan was saying when I approached. "It was an accident."

"Oh, really?" Rhys taunted. "So you're not still mad about what went down with Celina?"

Kellan scoffed. "If I was, I'd do more than spill a drink on you."

Rhys's hands curled into fists. "That a threat, Greene?"

Rhys formed essence in his hand, and I threw myself between the two of them. "Whoa, guys! Let's calm down."

"Take it outside!" one of Rhys's friends shouted. "We want to see a fight."

Kellan frowned. "We're not going to fight."

Rhys smirked. "Why not? You scared?"

Kellan didn't take the trash talk lightly. He chuckled and glared at Rhys like I wasn't standing right between them. "Scared for you, bro."

Rhys narrowed his eyes. "Ah, I see. You think you're some sort of hero after what you and your friends did. Why don't you prove it?"

"Screw you, Rhys," Kellan growled. "I don't have anything to prove to you."

Rhys's lips tightened, and I could tell he was getting more and more frustrated with Kellan by the minute. It was clear he was itching to start a fight.

"Enough," I stated firmly. "Kellan, we're leaving."

I grabbed Kellan by the arm and tried to drag him away, but we barely made it a step before Rhys said, "I see you need your girlfriend to keep you in check. Good luck with that mess."

Kellan wrenched his arm away from me and whirled on Rhys, getting so close their noses almost touched. "*Excuse* me?"

My jaw dropped. Did he just call me a *mess*? Who the hell was he to say that about me?

Rhys scoffed, and his eyes darted in my direction. "Come on, man. She's the one who exposed herself. She's the reason Annie got hurt and you had to launch your *rescue* mission. What's she going to do next? How many people are going to get hurt because of her?"

Kellan's hands balled into fists. "This isn't her fault. I'm alive because of her. No thanks to your skank girlfriend, who tried to kill Cora in that fire."

My eyes went wide. I didn't think until now that Kellan

believed me about what had happened before he'd arrived that night.

Rhys glared down at Kellan. "My girlfriend's a skank? What about yours? How many professors did she have to sleep with to get back into the academy after that disaster of a final?"

Kellan totally lost it. Before I could even react to Rhys's accusation, Kellan slammed his fist into the side of Rhys's face. I gasped as a cracking sound filled the air. Rhys formed another ball of essence in his hand and shot it at Kellan's face.

I reacted quickly and shot my own essence between them. My white essence collided with Rhys's black magic, and a loud *boom* sounded through the bar. A blast of air rushed through my hair, bur Rhys caught the brunt of the blow. Essence exploded in front of him, and he was blasted back into the table behind him, making the feet screech across the floor. Complete silence fell over the room as the whole bar turned to look at us.

I didn't care that everyone was watching. I stepped right up to Rhys, who looked down at me with a wary expression. It was like he thought I was going to slam essence in his face, and he knew he couldn't retaliate against a girl when everyone else was watching.

But I didn't touch him. Instead, I got up close in his face and sneered, "Believe me, you don't want to mess with us. You already know I'm not opposed to breaking the rules, so I suggest you don't test just how far I'd go to protect the people I love."

I whirled around, and Kellan was right there to catch

me. My heart was pounding fiercely as he took my hand in his and we made a dramatic exit together. Celina stood a few people back with drinks in her hands. She'd gone still in shock. Kellan and I rushed out of there so quickly that I accidentally shoved my shoulder into Celina's. She gave a yelp as her drinks splashed up on her shirt.

Kellan took long strides, so I had to practically run to keep up with him. But I didn't care. I wanted to get out of there as soon as possible.

Kellan didn't stop until we were outside and far away from the dining hall. A cold rain was sprinkling down on us, but Kellan didn't seem to care. He stood in front of the Winged Fountain, rainwater starting to drench his hair, and looked down at me. It was impossible to read his gaze. I didn't know if he was mad at me or proud. It might've been a little of both.

"Cora, I thought I told you last time not to get involved in stuff like this," he growled.

"I wasn't just going to stand there!" I shot back.

"You're making yourself a target," he insisted. "Rhys never would've said those things about you if you didn't confront Celina the last time."

"Those are just words," I argued, blinking away the rain from my eyes. Given the weather, I should've been shivering, but I was so worked up right now I barely noticed the chill.

"Words that *mean* something," Kellan said.

"He could've hurt you, too!" I shot back.

Kellan winced, like I'd hit a nerve. I glanced down to his hand—the one he'd used to punch Rhys—and my stomach bottomed out. Purple bruises had formed all over his knuckles.

My tone softened. "You did get hurt, didn't you? That crunch I heard…?"

Kellan cradled his broken hand to his chest. "I can deal with that. What I can't deal with is if you got hurt because of me."

I took a step forward. I longed to reach out for Kellan, but I hesitated. "Rhys wouldn't have hurt me."

"You don't know that," he said. "He thinks we're dating. If he wanted to hurt me, he'd go after you first."

"Why didn't you correct him then?" I asked.

Kellan opened his mouth to say something, but he shut it a second later. Finally, he said, "Would it matter? You're my partner. He'd hurt you either way."

"I can take care of myself," I said.

Kellan's eyes darkened. "So can I. I don't need you stepping in to deal with Celina and Rhys. In case you haven't noticed, I'm not completely helpless."

My heart sank. Is that what he thought it meant when I stood up for him? That I thought he was *weak*?

"I don't think you're helpless, Kellan," I stated. "That couldn't be further from the truth."

"Then what's your fascination with getting into trouble for me?" he snapped.

I gaped at him. "I don't have a fascination with it. Is this some male ego thing or something? Is this why you didn't tell me you were going after the Infantry and left me behind? Because you thought I might screw something up?"

"No!" he yelled. "I did that to protect you."

"You can't protect me from everything, Kellan. That's part of the job we're training for."

Kellan raked his fingers through his wet hair with his good hand. "Well, maybe this job is too dangerous."

The words felt like a slap in the face. It was like he was saying I wasn't cut out for this. I blinked away the water from my eyes as the rain picked up, but I couldn't help but glare at him. He didn't freaking own me. He couldn't tell me what to do. And so what if this job was too dangerous? I was doing it anyway.

Kellan must've noticed the hurt look on my face, because he stepped forward and softened his tone. "Cora, it's not like I don't think you can't do it. I just... I just couldn't stand to see you get hurt."

I swallowed, and my pulse quickened. He was so close now that I could feel the heat coming off his body. "Well, you're probably going to," I said. "Fighting fires is danger-ous, Kellan, but it's what I signed up for."

Kellan's features softened. He reached up to brush a few strands of wet hair behind my ear, and I gasped at the contact. "You'd do it with or without me, wouldn't you?"

I nodded, because I couldn't find my voice to answer. The way he looked down at me was so hypnotic.

"Then promise me one thing, Cora," he whispered.

"Anything," I replied breathlessly.

He stared with such an intense gaze it made my knees go weak. "Don't ever walk into danger without me."

I was shocked by the way he said it—like he never

wanted to leave my side. "I can't make any promises. Why do you care so much anyway?"

Kellan's lips tightened, like he didn't dare answer. "Did you mean what you said in Heaven's Lounge?"

"Did I mean what?" I asked.

"You told Rhys you'd do anything to protect the people you love," Kellan reminded me. "Did you mean it? Do you love me?"

I was blindsided by the question. So he'd caught that, had he? The words were heavy and light at the same time. I wanted so badly to tell him the truth—that yes, I loved him. But I didn't know if that was what he wanted to hear, and I couldn't risk screwing up our partnership.

"Cora, do you love me?" he asked more clearly, more firmly.

"I—I might. I mean, I think so," I stammered. "But you just broke up with Celina, and you got shot, and if you don't feel the same way, I understand—"

Kellan pressed his hand to the side of my face and stared deeply into my eyes. "You've got it wrong, Cora. The reason I can't stand to see you in danger is because… I feel the same way about you."

Without warning, Kellan's lips swooped down to connect with mine. The kiss was unlike anything I'd felt before. My body reacted before my head caught up with what was happening. My stomach flipped in my abdomen, and all the rain pounding down on us seemed to disappear. It felt as if the sidewalk had dropped away and we were floating in midair.

I realized what was happening and relaxed into the kiss.

As I wrapped my arms around him, he placed his good hand at the back of my neck and cradled me in his arms. Kellan's tongue rolled over mine, and he kissed me with a passionate energy that sizzled between us. It was as clear as when he siphoned my essence, but it was different. This energy went back and forth, instead of going in just one direction. It was something I received as much as I gave. It sucked the very breath from my lungs.

I thought kissing Kellan again would feel awkward. The first time I kissed him—right after we escaped from the fire—was anything but the passionate kiss our first kiss should've been. But this… this was different. This felt perfectly natural, even with the rain pouring down on us.

All too soon, Kellan drew away from me. My head was still spinning, and he inhaled deep breaths. Rain dripped down his face, but he didn't rush to wipe it away. I was frozen in place, still trying to wrap my head around Kellan's confession and the kiss.

Kellan stared down at me a moment longer, then wrapped me into a hug. He kissed the top of my head, and I suddenly felt more alive as my stomach flipped in my abdomen. Being in his arms felt perfect. I couldn't believe just months ago we were fighting about being partners. It felt like a lifetime.

"I don't want to keep fighting, Cora," Kellan whispered.

"I don't, either," I admitted. "But that means from here on out, we do things together. No running off without telling me."

"Deal," he said. "But you need to leave Celina and Rhys

alone. We have bigger things to worry about, and I don't need to worry about them fighting with you."

I drew away from him and nodded. "Agreed."

Kellan took my hand in his, and I squeezed his hands to let him know we were on the same page. Kellan winced, and my heart lurched. I jerked away from him immediately and threw my hands over my mouth.

"Oh my gosh! I'm sorry," I cried. "I forgot—"

"It's fine," Kellan said through gritted teeth.

I rolled my eyes at him. "No lying to me, either."

He smirked. "Well, I'm just going to omit how bad that hurt then."

"Come on, Kellan," I said. "Let's get you healed."

We started in the direction of the health services center. The rain had let up, and I wasn't sure if it was the weather or how I felt around Kellan, but I felt warmer now.

"Is this going to start becoming a habit?" I teased, glancing down to his hand.

Kellan followed my gaze and chuckled. "As long as we're partners? Probably."

My jaw dropped dramatically. "What does that mean?"

Kellan smiled and put his good arm around my shoulder. "It means we'll have lots of stories to tell."

Kellan wasn't lying when he said we had stories to tell. I wished they were the good kind—like sneaking into each other's dorms when our roommates were away. But between our classes and homework, we only had a few moments here and there to sneak kisses in the stairwell. Any time we had alone was spent on bigger problems—mainly, figuring out what to do about the threats mounting outside the academy.

"We have a plan," Kellan announced a few weeks later.

The two of us stood at the front of the study room we'd reserved in the library. The crew who'd helped break out Annie—along with Kumar, Laura, and Shaylene—sat crowded around the table.

"Perfect," Drew said, tapping his fingers on the tabletop. "What's the plan?"

Travis rubbed his hands together. "Yeah, are we going to burn their warehouse to the ground?"

"No," Kellan answered in a sharp tone, but he quickly clarified. "We don't want anyone else getting hurt."

"To be honest, I'm starting to wonder why no one else *has* gotten hurt," Shaylene pointed out. All eyes turned to her. "I mean, you stole their one bargaining chip. Why haven't they retaliated yet?"

"That's a good point," Kellan said, "and something Cora and I have been considering. Our best guess is they're planning something—something big."

Warner frowned. He was Kellan's roommate and hadn't been there the night of the rescue mission, but Kellan had managed to recruit him since. "I don't like the sound of that."

Kellan shook his head. "No, you shouldn't. But we have to be prepared for anything."

Kellan started passing out sheets of paper, while I stepped to the front of the room to explain.

"You all know that campus security has increased this semester," I said. "However, there are parts of campus that security doesn't have access to—namely, the students. We need eyes and ears everywhere. If you hear the slightest whisperings of a threat against campus—or against any of us—you report back to Kellan or me, and we'll relay the message to Chancellor Harris."

Kellan finished passing out the papers and stood beside me. "We've already talked with Chancellor Harris, and she's given us the go-ahead to form a student security team."

Caleb looked down at his paper. "The Supernatural Cavalry?"

Kellan shrugged. "Colt Walter has the Infantry. We'll fight them with the Cavalry."

Laura smiled. "I like it."

"These are your schedules," Kellan said, gesturing to the papers. "We've also emailed each of you a copy. We'll be patrolling areas campus security deems less important, like the dorms, dining hall, and the Activities Center."

Shaylene's jaw dropped. "Those are *less* important? There are students in those buildings all the time."

Kellan held up a hand. "I'm not saying security won't be there, but they've allocated their resources to the perimeter and classroom buildings—especially the Academy Building where all the administrative offices are."

Laura bit her lip while she looked over the schedule. "Do you really think the school is in this much danger?"

"We can't know for sure," Kellan said, "but we have to be prepared. The Infantry has shown they're capable of anything. In the meantime, I've spoken to my father about getting a meeting with the Alliance. We need to escalate this issue to the proper authorities."

Kellan's gaze flickered to mine. "My dad made it sound like what happened last semester is a hot topic within the council. Maybe we can leverage that somehow. What we need from you guys is help developing a presentation that will ensure the Alliance takes us seriously and we can implement the most effective solution."

"Hold up," Miles said, raising his hand. "Why wouldn't the Alliance take us seriously?"

Kellan frowned, and his eyes darted toward me. "Well, we're already in deep, with what happened during our final last semester. My dad says they've heard whisperings of our rescue mission, but luckily the Alliance doesn't know all the details."

"Luckily?" Tucker asked.

Kellan raised an eyebrow. "You think they wouldn't prosecute us for flying through the city that night? They have their suspicions from the rumors, but they can't confirm anything."

Kellan and I exchanged a glance, but it was me who spoke. "We think Chancellor Harris might be protecting you guys to keep from attracting any more attention to the academy."

"Okay," Travis said, clapping his hands together. "Let's get started."

After our meeting with the team, I was starting to feel more positive. There'd been no attack on the school, and I was starting to wonder if maybe Kellan's rescue mission had scared the Infantry off.

"You might be right," Kellan said to me before class one day. We were hiding in an alcove by the stairs, talking in hushed voices. "But I'm not ready to get my hopes up."

"You worry too much," I told him.

Kellan brushed my hair behind my ear, and tingles spread all the way down to my toes. He liked to siphon my essence every time he touched me just to make me jump a little. It got me every time.

"There's a reason for that," he whispered.

My heart pounded as Kellan leaned in. He brushed his lips across mine, and they tingled where he touched. I took his face in my hands and pulled him closer to me. His hands roamed over my back, and I arched my spine to press against him. Kellan's hand traveled down further and further, until he was cupping my ass.

I gasped, but I didn't pull away.

He chuckled and spoke between kisses. "You like that?"

"I like everywhere you touch me," I said breathlessly.

Kellan's gaze darted down to my breasts, then back up to my eyes. "I think we can steal a few hours after class. Warner's got security duty in the dining hall tonight."

Please, God. Yes! Kellan and I had hardly gotten to second base. I was dying for more, and I knew he was, too.

"We should probably get to class," I whispered.

Kellan faked a frown, then squeezed my butt again. "If I have to."

I snickered. "We don't really have a choice."

"We could skip," he suggested playfully.

"And fail the kidney section of the final?" I reminded him.

His shoulders fell. "Fine. Let's go."

We walked hand-in-hand to our human physiology class and sat beside each other. Celina and Rhys were at the front of the class. She kept shooting Kellan glances, but he was making it a point to ignore her. She was obviously bothered by it.

Whatever. Screw her. She didn't deserve a second of his attention.

None of our other friends had this class with us. They'd all been put in the other lecture block and were always a day ahead of us on material. Kellan and I silenced our phones, since Professor Braff has a strict no-phone-in-class policy.

Professor Braff strolled into the room a few minutes later. He was my anatomy professor last semester and still one of my favorite teachers. He gave a few students high-fives as he walked in, and Everett made a few jokes about Professor Braff's skeleton tie.

"Okay, okay, settle down," Professor Braff said, straightening his tie. "Last week, we left off with an overview of the kidneys. Today, we'll dig in deeper."

Professor Braff opened up his slideshow on the projector and showed us a diagram of the kidneys. He clicked a button on his computer, and the image zoomed in to a small structure inside the kidney labeled *nephron*. I started taking notes immediately.

"We all know that the kidneys filter the blood," Professor Braff started, "but they don't do it by magic. Each of our kidneys is made up of millions of small units called nephrons. These are the filtering units that take waste out of the bloodstream—"

The door burst open, cutting Professor Braff off. I jumped in my seat when I saw Shaylene grasping the door frame with tears streaming down her face. She gasped for breath, as if she'd been running. Her eyes scanned the room, until her gaze fell upon Kellan and me seated beside each other. My stomach plummeted to my toes.

Professor Braff's eyebrows knitted together. "Miss Hargrove?"

"Sorry, Professor," she said breathlessly. "I need to talk to—"

Kellan and I were already on our feet. We grabbed our coats and rushed out of the room. I grabbed Shaylene by the shoulder and dragged her down the hall, since she seemed too shocked to move herself.

"Shaylene!" I shook her, but her eyes glossed over. I was aware that the classroom door had been left open and students were talking indistinctly about the interruption. There were even a few people who stuck their heads out the door to see what was going on. But I didn't pay any attention to them.

Kellan stepped between Shaylene and the classroom door, so people wouldn't see her cry.

"Shaylene, what's wrong?" he demanded.

She blinked a few times, then wiped the tears away. "S-something's happened."

Shaylene held up her phone, and my guts twisted at what I saw. A video played across the screen. It shook a little, like someone recorded it on their phone. It showed six people on their knees in the middle of a tiled floor. The angle looked down on them, so we couldn't see behind them. Their hands were held up in surrender. Tears glistened in several of the girls' eyes, but the guys kept a stoic look on their face, like they weren't willing to show their emotions.

"Oh my God!" I cried. "Is that Laura and Travis?"

Shaylene sniffed. One of the guys lifted his head, and I

realize Caleb was there, too. I recognized the three other girls from my Art of Healing II lecture—Sarah, Avery, and Lisa. Laura sat still like Travis and Caleb, not giving her thoughts away.

Various sets of feet passed in front and behind them, encircling them like they were prey. We couldn't see their faces, but we could hear the indistinct voices of men whispering in the background.

"What is this?" Kellan demanded.

"It was sent to my ph-phone," Shaylene sniffled. "The three of them left a half hour ago with a group of girls who had to stop at the bank downtown. They were escorting them as part of the Supernatural Cavalry."

"Who sent the video?" Kellan growled.

Shaylene's bottom lip quivered. "It came from Caleb, but I-I think the guys who have them sent it, like they wanted me to see it."

Kellan and I glanced at each other, before realizing a second later we were in all their phones as contacts. We both scrambled to grab our phones out of our pockets. My body froze when I saw that I had messages from both Laura and Travis with a link to the video.

I glanced up to Kellan. "Do you think it's live?"

Kellan stared down at the video, his lips tightening with each passing second. "We better hope so. If we could only figure out where they're at..."

"I think they're still at the bank," Shaylene said. "When I first opened the video, I could see the teller windows in the background. But I don't know which one."

Kellan eyed the video a second longer. One of the men

stepped in front of the hostages. "Here's what's going to happen," he sneered.

The sinking feeling in my gut turned to stone cold rocks as I heard the sickening cold voice of Colt Walter play over the speakers.

"You're going to expose yourself for what you truly are," Colt said. I couldn't see his face, but I saw the gun in his hand. "Then the whole world will know the truth."

Travis's lips tightened. "You think we're going to give in that easily?"

Colt lifted his gun and pointed it at Travis's face. My whole body began to shake.

"You will… or the girl dies." Colt shifted his gun, and the barrel pointed directly between Laura's eyebrows.

The camera angle shifted to fit the gun into the frame, and we caught sight of the pillars and dark wood tones around the room.

Kellan inhaled a sharp breath. "I know this place. It's on Bleecker Street."

Shaylene's eyes lit up. "Then let's go!"

The three of us took off in the direction of the parking lot. Outside, the sky was dark with storm clouds. The video continued to play on our phones, and my lungs felt as if they were going to burst from holding my breath. Colt was still negotiating with Travis, but I worried he might pull the trigger at any second.

"Wait, wait!" I cried as soon as we stepped outside and I spotted the bell tower of the Academy Center in front of us. "We need to tell Chancellor Harris before we run off."

"You guys go!" Shaylene told us. "I'll talk to Chancellor Harris."

Shaylene ran off in the direction of the Academy Center, while Kellan started toward his car. I took quick steps beside him, but I didn't really watch where I was going. I couldn't tear my eyes from the video in front of me. Colt had Travis pinned to the floor now, the gun pressed against the back of his skull. Colt's face finally came into view, but it was covered by a ski mask.

"You know what you are!" Colt was yelling.

I tore my gaze away from the video. "Shit, Kellan. They're going to kill our friends."

"No, they're not." Kellan pulled his phone to his ear as he wrenched open the driver's side door.

"What are you doing?" I asked breathlessly.

Kellan's lips tightened. "Calling in the Cavalry."

As I slid into the passenger seat, he stuck his key into the ignition. He turned his attention from me to whoever was on the other line. "Warner? They've got six supernaturals at the bank on Bleeker. We're going to need all the help we can get."

"I'm on it," I heard Kellan's roommate say.

Kellan punched his screen to end the call. My heart slammed against my rib cage.

It'll all be fine, I told myself. *Colt can't get away with this...*

Unless he killed one of my friends first.

I couldn't bear to think of that.

Kellan drove so fast through the academy gates that security barely had a chance to buzz us out. Word of the video must've not reached the highest authorities at school yet, or the place would be on lockdown. Right now, that wouldn't stop Kellan or me, though. We had to get to our friends—immediately.

Kellan stepped on the gas and tore through a yellow light at the end of the street. He took sharp turns and weaved between traffic like he was on a freaking race-course. But I didn't care. I held on to the oh-shit handle and tried to keep my body from shaking as the video continued to play.

Colt ripped off Travis's shirt. "Show us! Show us who you truly are!" he yelled.

My eyes widened in horror. "Where's the Alliance!? They should be responding to this shit."

Kellan's eyes darkened, but he kept them on the road.

Another male voice came through the video. "They want to talk to you."

I glanced down to the video to see one of the masked men handing Colt a wireless landline phone. It must've been one of the bank's phones. Colt took it and walked off camera, until we couldn't hear him. Our fellow classmates didn't move, and the video had gone quiet.

"Why are they showing us this?" I demanded, though I didn't think Kellan knew the answer. "Do you think it's everywhere? If they want to turn people against us, why are they being total assholes?"

Kellan shook his head. "I think this is for us."

"To scare us?" I asked.

He took another corner and said, "Exactly."

We turned onto Bleecker street, and I was half terrified, half relieved by what I saw. Police cars were lined up in front of the bank a block away, and barricades had been set up to keep traffic from coming through. Their lights blinked on top of their vehicles, and police pointed their guns at the entrance of the bank. In front of the barricades, traffic cops were directing cars through a detour onto the next street.

I swallowed the lump in my throat. "They think it's a robbery."

There was nowhere for us to park, but traffic was backed up as it was, so Kellan just shoved the car into park, and the two of us jumped out of the car. We ran toward the barricades, but two cops jumped in front of us to stop us.

"I'm sorry," one of them said, "but we can't let you go any further."

"Our friends are in there!" I yelled at them.

The taller of the two puffed out his chest at me. "Miss, I'm going to have to ask that you stand back."

"We have information that could help," Kellan insisted.

"What kind of information?" the cop asked firmly.

"They want to negotiate," Colt's voice came through my phone.

I held up the video. "We know what's happening inside."

The cop's eyes narrowed on me, like he suspected I might have something to do with this. "We're going to have to show that to the chief."

He reached for my phone, but I jerked it away. "I want to talk to him."

When the officer hesitated, Kellan added, "We have more information."

We didn't. Not really. But the officer must've believed us, because he said, "Wait here just a moment."

The second officer kept watch on us while the first walked over to the police chief. The chief stood next to a team of high-ranking officers. One of them was on the phone, which I assumed was the negotiator who'd called the bank phone to talk to Colt. The chief looked surprised when the officer approached him, then glanced our way. His lips tightened, but he made his way over to us anyway.

"Hi, I'm Chief Brown," he said as he approached. He sounded distressed, but he tried to remain friendly. "I hear you have information that can help us."

I handed him my phone. "They're recording what's going on inside. Our friends are in there, and they sent links to our phones to make us watch."

The chief's eyes went wide as he stared at the video. It was hard to tell what was going on now, because whatever was happening was taking place off camera.

Kellan inhaled a sharp breath. It was so quiet that no one else noticed, but I did. When I glanced at him, I saw his eyes were locked on the police chief's vest. I followed his gaze and noticed a symbol on his clothing. It was an embroidered Alliance symbol—three hands linked together. I realized what it meant right away.

"Chief Brown," Kellan said quickly. "If it helps, our friends and us go to Harris Academy."

The chief's eyes snapped upward, and they flickered between the two of us. He didn't look at the other police officers when he addressed them. "Please give me a moment with these students, if you will."

"But sir—" one of them protested.

"I said I need a minute," he repeated.

The officers stepped away, and the chief leaned in and lowered his voice. "You're both one of them, aren't you?"

The way he said *them* suggested he wasn't supernatural at all. He was human, but the symbol on his shirt told us he knew our secret.

Kellan and I nodded in unison.

The chief's face paled, and he glanced back down to the video. In it, Colt was saying, "This isn't a negotiation. We're going with the plan and exposing them."

"This isn't a bank robbery, is it?" the chief asked.

"No," Kellan said. "These people followed our friends and cornered them here. They're trying to get our friends to expose themselves on camera."

The chief frowned. "This changes everything about our negotiation tactics. Is there anything else you can tell me?"

"The group calls themselves the Infantry," I said.

Chief Brown's eyes narrowed. "These people again?"

"You've heard of them?" Kellan sounded irritated.

"We're aware of the problems you've had at school," he said.

"Then why haven't you done anything?" Kellan demanded.

The chief ignored his question.

Colt's raging voice came through the video. "Tell us the truth!"

There was so much anger in his voice. I just didn't get what he was so mad about. I'd said it before, and this just confirmed it. Colt wasn't scared of us. Though he'd amassed a following of terrified people who wanted to know the truth, it was clear that wasn't Colt's motives. He already knew what we were. He wasn't using *his* fear against us. He was using everyone else's.

The only thing was, I couldn't figure out why. What did he have against us?

I heard the sound of Laura whimper, and that was my moment of clarity. I turned to Kellan. "Kellan, we have to talk to Colt."

"What? No," he insisted. Darkness crossed his features, like he thought this was one of those dangerous situations I promised I wouldn't get into anymore.

"Colt wants to know the truth, Kellan," I said. "We need to show him who we truly are."

Chief Brown cut in before Kellan could respond. "I'm sorry, but I can't let you speak to him while there are hostages in there."

"Cora, he already knows what we are," Kellan argued.

"He doesn't," I replied. "If he did, he wouldn't be doing any of this. He thinks we're something we're not. If we could just show him how good we truly are—"

"Cora, you promised." Kellan pressed his fingers to his eyes. "No more putting yourself in danger."

"I never promised that," I reminded him. "I only said I wouldn't do it without you."

Kellan's features softened.

"I'm sorry, but no," Chief Brown insisted.

"Please," I begged. "I can help."

Kellan grabbed my arm. "Cora, you can't."

I ignored Kellan. "Make him a deal," I said to Chief

Brown. "Let him take me in exchange for the other hostages."

"No!" Kellan cried. "If we're making exchanges, I'm going in."

I turned to Kellan. "We both know he's not going to make that deal with you. He's wanted me since the beginning."

Kellan's features were hard, but his expression wavered. He knew I was right.

"No one's going in there," Chief Brown insisted.

I crossed my arms. "Do you want to lose six people today? Ask for the exchange, and I guarantee he'll agree."

"I can't," he insisted again. "Why do you think you can talk him down? Do you have a personal connection with these criminals?"

Kellan and I exchanged a glance.

"Not really," I said.

"I really am sorry, kids," Chief Brown said regrettably. "But we're doing our best. I'm going to have to ask you to return behind the barricades and allow our officers to do their jobs."

"Of course," Kellan said, grabbing my arm tighter. "Thank you for your time, chief."

Kellan started dragging me away.

I ripped my arm out of his grasp. "Kellan, wait. We have to help! Our friends are in there!"

Kellan and I stepped to the other side of the barricade, and he whirled toward me, his nostrils flaring. There was a dark look in his eyes I'd never seen before. He pushed his fingers through his hair, then balled his hands into fists at his side. "I know, Cora. Believe me, I'm as pissed as you are. But we can't just run in there guns blazing."

"I'm not suggesting that," I said, though my eyes flickered upward.

Kellan noticed. "You're thinking of flying to the roof and seeing if there's a way in, aren't you?"

I crossed my arms. "Well, there has to be a back entrance somewhere."

"Or it's a bank and it's secure?" he retorted. "You don't think the police already have this place surrounded?"

"If we could just talk to him…"

"Then what?" Kellan pressed. "Cora, we don't want anyone getting hurt."

"People *are* getting hurt," I reminded him. "Kumar, Annie, all those people you went to the warehouse with. Kellan, if we don't do something, I'm afraid—"

Bang!

The sound of a gunshot rang through the street. My heart jumped and began racing a hundred miles per hour. Several people along the street screamed, and the chief started barking orders. Kellan grabbed me, and we ducked into a nearby alleyway.

Tears pricked at my eyes. "Oh my God! Do you think—?"

Kellan ripped his phone from his pocket and pulled up the video. My phone was still with the chief. He didn't let me look right away, until he breathed a sigh of relief.

"That was a warning shot," Colt's voice growled through the speakers.

My heart settled a little, but it was still racing. "Shit,

Kellan. He's not screwing around. The only reason he's holding out is because the police are outside. We have to do something!"

Kellan's hands shook, but he wouldn't show his emotions on his face. "I know, Cora. I just…"

"You just what?" I asked.

He took a breath. "I don't want you getting hurt, too."

I crossed my arms, but my heart was still racing. "You may have to accept that as a possibility. Unless…"

Something hit me.

"What?" Kellan asked.

"We don't have a way in there, but we *can* talk to Colt," I pointed out. "He has our friends' phones."

Kellan inhaled a sharp breath. "Good idea. But *I'm* doing the talking."

"Anything to get Colt to step down," I said.

Kellan brought up his contacts and punched a few buttons on the screen, then pulled the phone to his ear. Each passing second felt like an eternity.

Please don't kill my friends. Please don't kill my friends.

Kellan's teeth ground together. "The bastard's not picking up!"

"Try again," I insisted.

Kellan called Travis's phone again, and then a third time after that. Finally, someone picked up.

"What the hell do you want?" one of Colt's cronies barked into the phone.

"I want to speak to your boss," Kellan stated firmly.

"Why would he want to talk to you?" the voice demanded. "Who are you?"

"I'm the guy who's going to give him what he wants," Kellan said.

The phone went silent, and I held my breath. For a moment, I thought they'd hung up, and I dreaded what might come next.

Kellan mumbled under his breath. "This bastard better—"

I cut him off by placing my hand on his arm. We both knew that kind of language could get one of our friends killed. He unclenched his jaw, and a moment later, a voice came over the phone. I recognized it as Colt's.

"I hear you have a deal for me," he practically sang.

"I do," Kellan said. "This is Kellan Greene, and I'm an Aedes."

Colt's evil laughter ran through the phone. "Oh, I know who you are, Kellan. I've been following you and Cora since you exposed yourselves. That was clever, by the way, telling everyone it was a hoax. So, what's this deal you have for me?"

"My friends won't give you what you want," Kellan said. "Let them go, and you can have me. I'll do whatever you say."

"Kellan!" I cried, but he shot me a dark look. My guts twisted in my abdomen.

Colt chuckled. "Is that her?"

"You're not getting her," Kellan growled. "You can have me. Just don't hurt my friends."

"Put your girlfriend on the phone, and I'll consider the deal," Colt replied.

Kellan hesitated. We both knew if we refused, we risked our friends getting hurt.

Colt spoke in a harsher tone. "Put her on the phone."

"Kellan, I've got this," I told him, reaching for the phone in his hand.

Kellan's nostrils flared, but he let me take it.

"I'm here," I said to Colt. "Look, all we want is our friends to be let go."

Colt chuckled. "And you know what happens the second I do that? The police come swarming in on all sides. I don't think so."

"Then what do you want, Colt?" I asked gently, though my hands were shaking in rage.

"I want everyone to know what you truly are," Colt said. "I want your kind to pay for what you've done."

"What is it that we've done?" I asked him.

"Like you don't already know," Colt sneered.

"I don't," I swore. "I'm sorry if one of us hurt you, Colt, but you have to know—"

"Hurt me?" he snapped. "Hurting me would've been preferable, little demon."

My guts twisted into a knot. It was obvious by the way he spoke that my theory was correct. He was *angry*—but angry at what, I didn't know.

"What happened to you?" I asked.

Colt laughed again, a laugh that sent a chill down my spine. "All you demons are the same—playing stupid when you know damn well what you've done! You took her from me! You took her!"

The phone shook in my hands. I knew now more than ever, saying the wrong thing would have dire consequences. And so, I had to make the best assumption I could.

"You loved her a lot, didn't you?" I tried my best to keep the shakiness from my tone.

"Of course I loved her," Colt snapped. "We were engaged. Your kind changed all that."

My pulse quickened. I had to keep Colt talking, to get him to tell me the rest of the story, but I had no idea where he was going with this.

"She got involved with the supernaturals, didn't she?" I asked, making the vaguest assumption I could.

"*She* got involved?" he balked. "More like *they* got involved."

"Involved how?" I asked. I didn't know how else to phrase the question, considering how little he was telling me.

"She was supposed to live!" he yelled.

That's when it hit me. He blamed *us*, the people who were supposed to heal his fiancé, for her death.

"Healing is a difficult process, Colt," I found myself saying.

"Healing?" he scoffed. "That's what you think you do?"

I furrowed my brow. "What do *you* think we do?"

"I know the truth," Colt growled. "After the accident, she was brought to the hospital and promised she'd make it. But I saw what those assholes with the winged emblem on their coats did. They drew her soul straight out of her body. I saw it. Seconds later, she went into a seizure, and she was dead before I could get the *real* doctors there."

I covered the phone's mouthpiece with my hand and looked to Kellan. "He thinks they took her *soul*. It makes no sense..."

Kellan looked as confused as I did.

I brought the phone back to my face. "What did her soul look like?"

"I don't know," Colt snapped. "Like all souls. White and glowing. You should know!"

My eyes widened, and Kellan had the same expression on his face. *Essence!* Colt had seen essence. My mind flickered back to one of our lessons earlier this semester. Professor Kovski had taught us about channeling, a technique where you place essence into someone's body to stabilize them until you can administer a transfusion or other care. What he must've walked in on was them removing the essence—but she wasn't stable enough yet and she had a bad reaction.

"I looked into the supernaturals after that," Colt continued, his voice getting angrier by the second. "I saw the emblem on their jackets, and I knew something was suspicious about Harris Academy."

"You have to know that's not what happened to her, Colt," I stated. "We're healers. They were trying to *heal* her."

He scoffed. "If that were true, why isn't she here right now?"

"Sometimes we can't heal everything," I said regrettably.

"You're right," he sneered. "You can't heal everything. Maybe your kind needs a taste of what it feels like to have a soul taken from you."

Sarah pleaded in the background. "No, please, don't! I'm just—"

Bang!

Cries reached my ears through the phone, and my whole body stilled.

"*Go, go, go!*" I heard the sound of Chief Brown's orders from down the street.

I couldn't move. I couldn't breathe. The last gunshot felt so uncertain. This one needed no confirmation. I knew he'd shot her.

It felt like all my insides were being pushed up through my throat, and my knees buckled beneath me. Kellan grabbed me before I dropped to the pavement. The line had gone dead, and the phone dropped from my hands.

Above us, the dark storm clouds finally gave way, and rain began to fall around us. It was slow at first, just small drops tickling the back of my neck, but the rain quickly picked up speed, until it was pounding down on us. Wind whipped through the alleyway, and hail pummeled the pavement. It might've hurt—if I could feel anything at all. But I'd gone numb to everything but the heat.

There was so much heat—anger and grief all rolled into one. It started in my eyes as the tears spilled over, then spread through my whole body like a raging inferno. My element was rising to the surface, and I couldn't control it. Raindrops sizzled on my skin.

Kellan cradled me in his arms, rocking me back and forth as tears streamed down my face.

"Oh, God," I sobbed, my shoulders shaking. "He... he... because of me."

"No." Kellan ran his fingers through my wet hair. "This isn't your fault, Cora. This is his fault and his fault alone."

"But if I hadn't insisted we call—"

"Then things could've turned out worse," Kellan said. I couldn't tell if he meant it, or if he was just saying that to make me feel better.

Except nothing could make me feel better right now. This wasn't a *feel better* kind of situation.

This was a moment to grieve.

a darkness took over the academy the following week. I barely remembered how we'd gotten back to the academy after the gunshots. It felt like one minute I was sitting out in the rain, and the next I was being piled under a layer of warm blankets.

He shot Sarah. He killed her.

And it was my fault.

"There's nothing more we can do," Kellan assured me when I insisted we go back.

But I knew he was already forming some sort of plan in his mind.

Colt had escaped. It was all over the news. I didn't know how he'd done it—and the police were still baffled—but he managed an escape and hadn't been heard from since. The police caught his cronies and rescued our friends. I couldn't have been more relieved to see Travis, Caleb, and Laura after everything that happened, but things were different. When Laura and I were alone in our room, she barely spoke. I knew it had to be from the trauma she'd experienced, but I worried that on some level she blamed me like I blamed myself. Her parents had come to visit, but she assured them she wanted to finish the semester. I had a feeling that had something to do with staying close to Travis.

There'd been a memorial service for Sarah in the auditorium. Kellan held my hand the whole time, but he kept glancing around like he thought Colt might show up after what he did to her. Nothing happened during the memorial service, and it felt as if nothing happened the days following. No one really spoke, in my classes or in the common areas. It was like we all felt the weight of what happened to Sarah and knew it could've been any one of us.

"I had the opportunity to meet with the Alliance this past week, and they're doing the best they can," Kellan announced one afternoon when the Supernatural Cavalry got together in our dorm's rec room. There was something in his voice, however, that suggested the Alliance hadn't been doing enough.

I glanced to Kumar, who sat straight in one of the plush chairs and looked very interested in what Kellan had to say. Kumar hadn't said anything about the shooting to me, but I could see it in his eyes—he knew Annie had been close to meeting the same fate as Sarah. Annie had gone home in Colorado, but I could see the fight burning bright in Kumar's eyes.

Kumar's hands tightened into fists. "They haven't caught Colt yet."

"No," Kellan confirmed, his lips pressed into a thin line. "They got some names, but we have no way of knowing how many there are. They're spread everywhere, but it's almost like…"

"Like what?" I asked.

Kellan pressed his lips together. "Well, I don't know for sure, but my dad made it sound like things aren't adding up. Records have already gone missing."

"We better hope they caught enough of them," Travis growled. "Without his people, Colt's on his own."

"Does that make him less of a threat?" Laura asked, twisting her hands in her lap.

Kellan's jaw tensed. "I would think so. Luckily, finals week is upon us. We just have one week of protecting the students, then everyone will be back home for the summer. We can hope the Alliance will catch Colt before school starts up again."

Travis groaned and got to his feet. "Man, I don't know how you stay positive all the time."

Kellan wasn't being positive. I could see it in his eyes. He felt terrible about what had happened and was only saying what he had to because everyone looked up to him.

"We should be out there hunting this guy down," Travis said.

Caleb stood beside him and cracked his knuckles. "I'd like to break my knuckles on that fucker's face."

Shaylene pressed a hand to Caleb's chest and spoke gently. "Believe me, we all want to see Colt pay for what he did, but we can't stoop to his level. We're better than that."

"Yeah," Caleb agreed. "We *are* better than that. I'm not

going to murder the bastard. I'll let the justice system take care of that."

"And we will," Kellan said. "In the meantime, we still have a school to protect until Colt is caught."

"I want to help," a female voice said in the doorway.

Everyone turned to see Celina standing there. I was so used to seeing Rhys at her side that I was kind of surprised to see her alone. On instinct, I stepped in front of Kellan, but he gently took my shoulder and pushed me aside.

"You what?" Kellan asked Celina.

"I want to help," she repeated.

Or you could go drown in a river, I thought. But instead, I said, "What makes you think we'd trust you?"

Celina stepped further into the room and crossed her arms. "Because this isn't about me and Kellan. This is about all of us. I don't want anyone else getting hurt, either."

I eyed her up and down, feeling my fire warm my skin in disdain. "Why the sudden change of heart? You've hurt enough people."

Warner put his hand over his mouth. "Oooh…"

Celina shot him daggers. "Do you want more help, or do you want to fight a second war with me?"

Kellan narrowed his gaze at her. "You know what? I want to hear it. Why should we trust you?"

Celina's lips pressed into a thin line. "You shouldn't."

When she saw the look of shock on our faces—we never thought she'd admit it—she sighed and added, "I mean, you're right. I haven't given you a good reason in the past to trust me, and I don't have a good reason now. All I can ask is that you take a chance."

Kellan eyed her a moment longer, his eyes darkening with each passing second. "Sorry, Celina, but I can't do that."

Her eyebrows shot up. "You can't—?"

"I can't take a chance," he said, shocking me a little.

"But all I want to do is help!" Cora pointed out.

"We have enough people," Kellan said. "And I trust them."

He emphasized it like he didn't trust Celina—and never would.

"Kellan, come on," Celina begged. "My essence is really strong. I can help."

Kellan's fists tightened at his sides, but his expression read pain. "You want me to trust you, Celina? Then you're going to have to earn that trust back." He eyed her up and down before adding, "Good luck with that."

Celina's jaw dropped as Kellan turned away from her. "Kellan? Kellan!"

He ignored her, and she huffed and stomped away.

Kellan pressed his fingers to his eyes when she left the room, like he couldn't stand one more thing. He sighed, then turned back to the group. "Everyone's got this week's schedule, right?"

"Yep," Warner said, waving his phone with his email open.

"Okay," Kellan said, sounding defeated. "We'll meet again on Wednesday."

Everyone started gathering their things and left the room, until just Kellan and I were alone. He stood by the window and looked outside. The sun had dipped below the walls of the academy half an hour ago, and night was starting to settle over campus.

I wrapped my arms around him. "It's going to be okay," I whispered, though I didn't feel it myself.

With Colt still out there and his sights set on the academy, I was constantly alert. Until he was caught, I wouldn't feel safe. The only solace was knowing that by the end of this week, campus would be empty and our classmates would be back home. In the back of my mind, I knew that didn't mean anything for me—Colt had already attacked my family and could do it again. But at least everyone else would be out of his clutches.

Kellan ran a hand across mine, but he didn't say anything. I could sense the tension in his body.

"I'm sorry about Celina," I whispered. He didn't talk about it much, but I could tell he was still upset about it.

He turned around and took my hands. "Don't worry about her."

Kellan wrapped me in his arms, and I laid my head on his chest, enjoying the rise and fall of his chest.

"This past week has been…" I trailed off.

Kellan ran his hands up and down my back, and some of the tension eased from my shoulders. "Crazy. I know."

"We need a vacation," I teased.

Kellan chuckled lightly. "Believe me, I've been thinking about it."

"Well, maybe once this is all over, we'll take a trip this summer," I said.

Kellan stilled. It hit me only a moment later what I'd

suggested. We hadn't even slept together yet, and already I was suggesting we take a vacation together.

I drew away from him. "I didn't mean—"

"No," he said with a shrug. "I think I'd like that."

My eyebrows shot up. "Really?"

He nodded and gave a shrug, as if to ask why not.

My heart lifted. "Where would you want to go?"

"Somewhere warm…" Kellan stared down at me with soft eyes, then pressed his lips to mine. The rec room spun around me. "And romantic."

"Mm…" I mused. "Romantic sounds nice. We've barely had a moment alone since we got together."

Kellan's lips twitched at the corners as his eyes roamed over my face. My chest warmed at the way he looked at me, and all I wanted to do was press my body closer to his.

"We need to do something about that," he suggested.

My eyes flickered down to his muscled chest. "Believe me, I want to. But you have Cavalry duty tonight."

Kellan frowned. "Damn… Do you want to join me?"

"Of course," I said, before I realized what his suggestion might mean. My heart beat wildly in my chest, because part of me wanted to take him up on the offer, while the other part reminded me nothing good could come from distracting him. "Wait. You don't mean…?"

Kellan laughed lightly and brushed my hair behind my ear. My skin tingled from where he touched me. "Is that what you want?"

My knees went weak when he suggested that. "Yes," I admitted. "But…"

"But…?" Kellan encouraged.

I sighed. "I thought things would be different, you know? That things wouldn't be all… crazy when we finally got together."

Kellan smirked. "That must be it."

"What?" I asked.

"We're cursed," he said simply.

I rolled my eyes. "You're right. That must be it."

Kellan's tone softened as he became serious again. "If that's what you want, Cora, then we'll wait."

"Hold on," I teased. "You, the *man*, are suggesting we wait?"

Kellan shrugged, but he looked uncomfortable, like what I said bothered him. "I just want it to be special for you… For both of us."

My heart melted. "I do, too. It almost seems… unfair, doesn't it?"

"What does?" he asked curiously, running his fingers across my collarbone as he stared down at me.

I dropped my head. "It's unfair that life keeps going on as normal for us after what happened. Sarah's gone, and Annie… well, she'll never be the same. Laura, either. She's been really quiet since it happened. I want to help, but I don't know how because she won't tell me how she feels."

Kellan pressed his lips together in thought. "You know what? You're right."

I raised an eyebrow. "That life's unfair? Yeah, I've kind of got the message since my mom was caught in an arson explosion."

Kellan's shoulders fell. "Exactly."

My stomach sank. "If you're trying to make me feel better, it's not working."

"No, I'm just saying... we don't really know what our friends went through in that bank," Kellan pointed out. "I think we should do something for them before the end of the semester."

The tension in my shoulders eased. "That's a really good idea, Kellan. I think it would make us all feel better. It will help to focus on something else."

"So, what should we do?" Kellan asked.

I smiled for the first time all week. "You let me take care of that."

18

"There," I said, putting the finishing touches on the snacks I'd lain out on my study desk. I took one of the chips from the bag and scooped up some dip with it, then popped it in my mouth. I turned to Kaylee, who was lying on my bed. "Thanks for bringing all this."

Kaylee smiled. "What are friends for?"

I hadn't left the academy all week, but Kaylee had agreed to go shopping for me, and received clearance from campus security since she was a Davina.

I walked over to her and wrapped her in a hug. "I'm so glad you're back from Europe. I can't wait to hang out with you this summer."

"I know," she said. "It's been so long."

I plopped down on the bed beside her.

Kaylee sat up straight. "I have a surprise for you."

"You do?" I asked.

She beamed. "I didn't want to tell you over the phone."

"What is it?" I begged. It sounded like good news.

"I applied for next semester," Kaylee said. "I got in!"

"Oh my God!" I cried, squeezing her into another hug. "That's great."

"I know," she enthused. "Europe was *amazing*, but I'm ready to get back to my studies. And I missed you so much."

I nudged her in the side and teased, "You're just eager to meet all the hot guys who go here."

She chuckled. "Maybe…"

We shared a laugh, but it was short-lived. There was a coolness in the air that hadn't left for days. I had a feeling we could both sense it.

I sighed and leaned against her. "I really missed you, Kaylee. When you're here, it's like I can forget all the craziness that happened this semester."

Kaylee wrapped an arm around me. "Do you want to talk about it?"

I shook my head, but inside, my guts were twisting. "Not really. People will be here soon."

"Right," she said. "Well, if they're not here in the next ten minutes, I'm going to eat all those chips."

"Go ahead," I replied. "You're the one who bought them."

The sound of footsteps met my ears, and I sat up straight. Laura stopped in our open doorway and glanced around at all the food and the TV set up with video games. She furrowed her brow as she stepped inside.

I jumped to my feet. "Surprise!"

Laura's features softened. "We're having a party?"

"Yep," I said. "To celebrate the end of finals. I thought

it'd be fun to play games and hang out before we all leave for the summer. Everyone else will be here soon."

For the first time all week, Laura cracked a smile. "I think that's a great idea, Cora."

Her eyes flickered to Kaylee on my bed, and I remembered the two had never met before.

"Laura, this is Kaylee, my friend from high school," I introduced. "Kaylee, this is Laura."

Kaylee stood and shook Laura's hand. "I've heard a lot about you."

"You, too," Laura said.

Kaylee's eyes lit up. "I hear you're the fashion expert around here. Do you think you could give me some pointers on my summer style?"

I'd told Kaylee my whole idea for the night was to get everyone's mind off what had happened. I had a feeling she made the suggestion to help Laura feel better, but I also knew the two would get along.

"Just summer?" Laura asked as she set her backpack at the foot of the bed. "We can come up with a plan for next fall, too."

"Really?" Kaylee seemed excited. "Fall's my favorite."

Laura reached for her stack of fashion magazines on her dresser. "Fall is gorgeous around here."

"Right?" Kaylee sat beside Laura on her bed, and the two started flipping through magazines.

Less than a minute later, Kumar stuck his head in the doorway. "I hear there's a party in here."

"Come in," I said, gesturing him inside.

"I brought the booze," he sang, holding two packs of beer above his head.

Kaylee lifted her head, and her gaze stopped dead on Kumar. He caught her eye and froze in place. Laura and I both chuckled, bringing them both back to reality.

Kumar set the beer on the floor and cleared his throat. "I don't believe we've met."

Kaylee giggled, like Kumar was being particularly charming. "I'm Kaylee, Cora's friend from high school."

"Well, hello, Kaylee, Cora's friend from high school. I'm Kumar, Cora's friend from college." He offered a light smile, which was promising, because I hadn't seen him smile at all after what happened to him and Annie.

To say that Kaylee fit in with my group at college was an understatement. As more people arrived, it was clear Kaylee was the missing puzzle piece in our whole gang. She got along with everyone great.

Everyone seemed to be having a great time hanging out, and it put me at ease. Laura and Shaylene leaned against a huge pile of pillows on Laura's bed and flipped through magazines together, while Kaylee and Kumar flirted in the corner and bonded over their love of snack food. Travis, Caleb, and Warner were laughing in front of the TV while they played a racing game on the video game console Kellan had loaned me. The rest of the guys—Drew, Miles, Everett, Jett, and Tucker—had set up their empty beer cans in the hall and were taking turns rolling a basketball at them.

Kellan and I sat on the bed and leaned against the wall. His arm wrapped around me, and my head lay on his chest.

"Why so glum?" he asked softly, so no one else could hear.

I looked up into his eyes. "I'm not glum."

"You're... quiet," he pointed out.

"I'm just enjoying seeing everyone having fun," I said.

He squeezed me tighter. "You did a good job. I think this is just what we all needed to end the semester with."

"How'd your finals go?" I asked.

Kellan smirked. "You're supposed to be taking your mind *off* things, Cora."

I chuckled lightly, but it felt forced. While I watched everyone enjoy their night, I was reminded of what had happened and everything that brought us to this moment.

"I'm trying," I told him honestly. "I just think... we all need more time."

"Agreed," Kellan said, running his fingers up and down my arm. Tingles spread across my skin. "No matter how long it takes, Cora, I'll be here to help you through it."

My heart melted in my chest. It was obvious I was taking everything harder than him, but I stared into his eyes anyway and added, "I want to be there for you, too."

He brushed my hair out of my eyes and looked at me like I was the only girl in the room. The sounds of the guys playfully yelling at each other in front of the TV and the girls giggling at magazines across the room seemed to fade when he gazed at me like that. I relaxed into him.

"We will, Cora," he whispered. "We'll always be there, no matter what happens."

I forced the corners of my lips into a slight smile. "Because we're partners."

Kellan shook his head. "No. Because we love each other."

Then his lips came down to meet mine, and I was totally swept off my feet. The room spun around me, and the words he'd just said echoed in my mind.

We love each other.

In that moment, I actually thought everything would be okay from here on out.

I drew away from the gentle kiss, my heart beating rapidly against my rib cage. "I love you, too, Kellan," I whispered, running my hand across his chest. "No matter what."

Our beautiful moment came to a screeching halt when the sound of Celina's voice came from down the hall. "Thank God!" she cried. "You have to come quick."

The sound of beer cans knocking over met my ears, but it was followed by a moment of complete and utter silence. Travis pressed pause on the game, and everyone stilled.

"What's happened?" Drew demanded from out in the hall.

Kellan jumped to his feet and rushed outside the room, and I hurried behind him.

Celina sucked in a deep breath, like she'd been running. "I was leaving the Academy Center, and I swear I saw him."

Kellan stepped forward and spoke in a firm voice. "Saw who?"

Celina's face paled. "Colt."

My heart lurched in my chest, and a wave of heat washed over my skin. "He's on campus?"

"But how?" Drew asked.

Celina ignored his question and answered mine first. "I

don't know for sure... He was wearing a hood, but I swear..."

She choked up a little. As much as I didn't like Celina—and didn't trust her—I had to believe she was telling the truth. She wasn't *that* good of an actress. By now, everyone else had come out of the room to see what was going on.

A muscle popped in Kellan's jaw, and he started down the hall without asking any further questions. "Come on, Cavalry. It's time to fight."

Kellan walked so fast that I had to take two steps for every one of his. My heart beat fast as I tried to keep up, and I felt as if a pile of bricks had just landed on me. This was bad. This was very bad.

But how did Colt get in? Security was all over the place.

"Wait," I said, turning to Celina, who had followed close behind. "Why'd you come to us first?"

"I didn't," she snapped. "I went straight to Chancellor Harris, *then* came here. If you think I'm lying—"

"It doesn't matter," Kellan said firmly. "We can't take any chances. But I swear on my very essence, Celina. If you're lying—"

"I'm not!" she insisted. "I told you the truth. I want to help."

Kellan eyed her a second longer, but must've decided there wasn't any time to waste, because he turned from her and said, "Fine. Let's go help security find this bastard."

Kellan took the steps at the end of the hall two times faster than I could. Everyone followed behind us, while Kellan barked orders. "Kumar, Caleb, Shaylene, and

Everett, you take the West wing of the first floor. Miles, Tucker, Travis, and Laura, the East wing…"

His instructions faded as I raced out of the building behind him. I could hardly process what he said as my pulse pounded in my ears.

It's happening again. Colt's going to hurt somebody.

I wasn't going to let that happen.

It was dark outside, with nothing more than the street-lamps around campus to light our way. When we reached the Academy Building, there was already a large group forming outside the doors. People flooded out from all entrances.

"They're being evacuated," Kellan stated, but he didn't slow his step.

He pushed through the crowd, and we all followed behind.

"Rhys!" Celina shouted as she met up with him.

He wrapped her in his arms. "I'm so glad you're okay. Your message was terrifying."

We reached the front, where a group of security officers were pushing people back away from the doors. Two officers held up their hands when Kellan tried to get through.

"This building's on lockdown," one of them stated firmly.

"We're here to help," Kellan said. "We're an official student security group, approved by the Chancellor herself."

"I'm under strict orders not to let anyone pass," the officer emphasized. "I don't care who you are."

The officers pushed the group back further into the

courtyard, until some were standing as far back as the Winged Fountain. Most people kept their distance, as they sensed something was wrong and dangerous.

Kellan's hands curled into fists. "We have to help! We can't just stand here."

The other officer stepped forward. "Standing back is the best help you can be right now."

I glanced through the glass doors, my heart pounding. I feared what I might see behind them. Instead of seeing Colt, though, I spotted Chancellor Harris standing beside her husband, Kane Harris, and a group of guys in fancy black suits. I recognized one of them as John Maddox, the public relations officer from the Alliance.

"What's the Alliance doing here?" I demanded.

I kept my eyes on Maddox. He took Chancellor Harris by the elbow and led her and the other Alliance members down the hall, toward one of the exits I couldn't see from here.

The officer ignored my question. "If you'll all please step back."

"What's the Alliance doing here?" I repeated, more firmly this time.

The officer pressed his lips together, looking displeased at my persistence. "It's nothing more than a regularly scheduled meeting with the school board," he answered, like that was supposed to ease my nerves about what was happening. "We're going to ask that you return to your dorms—"

Boom!

A deafening sound filled the air, so loud that it made

my ears ring. I felt the shock wave move through my body, and I was thrust backward by the force of the blow. On instinct, my wings tore through my shirt, and I thrust them out on either side of me to slow my momentum. Still, I landed hard on the ground and gasped for breath.

I couldn't hear the screams over the sound of the crumbling building. My vision blurred, but it barely registered as reality came crashing down on me.

The academy center had just been bombed.

Colt Walter had just launched an attack on the school.

19

"Cora!"

Someone shouted my name, but I didn't hear who. My ears were still ringing, and when I tried to push myself to my feet, the world spun around me, and I was back on the ground again in less than a second.

"Cora!"

The voice came again, and I was suddenly aware of hands grasping my shoulders. I looked up into the face of the man shouting my name, but I couldn't focus on it. The streetlamps had flickered out above our heads, which left only the moonlight casting shadows across his face.

Essence whipped through my body, and my vision began to clear. Kellan's pale face swam in front of me, but I finally planted my feet firmly and saw him clearly. Color filled his cheeks as he drew more and more essence from me and into himself. Energy sizzled through me as I came back to reality, but my gut sank the moment everything came together.

"Oh my God!" I gasped.

The West wing of the Academy Center was in total shambles. It was nothing more than a pile of bricks. Parts of the East side still stood, but windows had been blasted out, and it looked like nothing more than a shell of the beautiful building that once stood there.

Screams filled the air around us, and I whirled around to assess the damage. Bricks and glass had been thrown into the crowd, and people were reeling on the ground in pain. Travis was knelt over Laura, who didn't look hurt but was a little out of it. Caleb had a huge gash on the side of his face from a shard of glass, and Shaylene was helping him heal it. Several of the guys had already jumped to their feet and were springing into action, while some of the crowd had scattered. Nearby, the blast had sent Warner into a tree, and he cradled his broken arm to his chest.

Panic hit me, but I pushed it aside. Now wasn't the time to get emotional. I knew that from my emergency training. Right now, I had to act.

I ran over to Warner and dropped to my knees beside him. "Kellan and I can help—"

"Forget about me!" Warner cried. "Help the people trapped in the building!"

He pointed toward the Academy Center.

Shit. He was right.

"We'll be back for you," Kellan told Warner.

"Go!" Warner shouted.

Kellan and I raced toward the Academy Center. The rubble was so thick that I didn't know how we were ever going to get down there.

"Shit!" Celina cried from beside me. I hadn't even noticed she and Rhys were behind us until she spoke. "We're going to need Earth Davina over here to move this stuff!"

Travis and Laura came up behind them. "We're right here," Travis said. "But it's going to take more—"

Boom!

We all jumped as a second explosion went off. It wasn't as close this time, but it made my heart jump into my throat nonetheless. We all whirled in the direction of the deafening noise, only to see the white bricks of the campus boundary walls crumbling in on themselves. Before the smoke even cleared, hordes of shadows appeared through the wreckage. There must've been hundreds of people stepping over the rubble to get inside the school.

We all exchanged a look of utter shock. What the hell was going on here?

"This world is ours, demons!" one of the Infantry members shouted. "Go back to hell, bitches!"

Rhys cracked his knuckles. "Let's get those motherfu—"

Bang. Bang. Bang.

The sound of gunshots rang out over campus. It was so loud and constant that it sounded like a warzone. On instinct, we all ducked behind the rubble. Screams echoed off what remained of the boundary walls. I peeked over the top of the pile of bricks we hid behind, my heart racing. The gunfire was evident against the dark of night, and thick balls of essence, both light and dark, whizzed through the air. Supernaturals had taken to the sky to escape the attack, but the men with guns turned their aim skyward. Several Aedes and Davina spiraled out of the air. All around us, the ground began to shake, and whirlwinds stirred as Davina began to use their elements to fight back. But the Infantry retaliated so quickly and without regard that our fellow students and faculty members fell quickly.

"Oh, God!" Shaylene cried as she and Caleb ran over to us.

The rest of our group gathered around quickly and hid themselves with us in the rubble. Kaylee crouched beside me, with Kumar pressed up close next to her. Warner sucked a sharp breath through his teeth as he leaned up against a pile of bricks.

"Hey, dude," Miles said, shooting glances between Warner and the Infantry. "Can we help with that?"

"Help them!" Warner insisted.

Kellan jumped immediately into leader mode. "Davina, you're going to have to use your elements. Drew, see if you can knock some guns out of their hands with your air."

Rhys's features darkened as he glanced toward the advancing Infantry members. He nudged Celina in the side. "Let's burn these assholes."

"No!" Kellan barked.

Rhys looked him up and down. "Why not?"

Kellan took a few ragged breaths, and his eyes darted to Shaylene, then Laura, before finally falling on me. "Because if we aim to kill, it makes us no better than them."

"You're wasting time!" Rhys growled.

Kellan shook his head firmly. "This isn't the way super-naturals fight. We're healers."

I was shocked to hear him say it. He gave me this look

like… I don't know… like something I'd said or done had changed his mind.

"Screw this," Rhys muttered, getting to his feet. "Let's go get them, Celina."

Celina hesitated and glanced between Rhys and the rest of us.

"You can't be serious!?" he roared.

Celina frowned. "I'm not a killer."

Rhys stared down at her a second longer, before scoffing and turning away. He jumped over the pile of rubble and raced away, dark essence forming in his palm. The tension in the air was palpable, but none of us had a moment to dwell on it. The Infantry were moving across campus quickly.

Celina pressed her lips into a thin line, as if trying to hide the way she felt about Rhys running off.

"You with us?" Kellan asked her.

She swallowed, then nodded firmly. "We stand together as one."

I never thought I'd ever see Celina take the school motto so seriously. She always seemed like the *I stand with you as long as you serve me* kind of girl. But she was serious about this. As Celina went silent, the obvious hurt on her face became evident. Rhys's departure was a betrayal—a clear end to their relationship. And yet, she chose standing beside us over him. She truly wanted to fight alongside us.

I held my hand out, palm to the ground. "We stand together as one," I repeated.

All hands came in to stack on top of mine, and the

group repeated the school motto in unison. "We stand together as one."

"Let's do this," Kellan said in an encouraging tone. He turned to Kaylee. "You're water, right?"

"Yes," she answered breathlessly as the sound of gunshot continued to ring out, closer now more than ever.

"Make it rain to distort their vision." Kellan turned to me. "Celina, Cora, and Caleb, we need to create a barrier with your fire. Travis and Laura, we need you on the offense."

Travis gave him a salute. "On it, bro."

"Everyone else knows what to do." Kellan nodded toward the remaining guys, and they took off running. They zig-zagged between piles of rubble to get closer and start throwing their essence at the men across campus.

Kumar placed his hand on Kaylee's shoulder. "I'm on your team, okay?"

She nodded firmly. "Got it."

Kaylee aimed her hands at the sky, while Kumar opened her essence channel to make her stronger. Dark clouds swirled above us, blocking out the stars.

Celina looked over the rubble, her eyes darting every which way. I could tell what she was thinking immediately. There were Aedes and Davina running everywhere. Most of them were too distracted to use their elements, but I feared we'd hurt our own if we started firing at will.

"We need to get closer," I barked.

"I've got you!" Laura yelled. "Kellan, some help?"

Kellan took Laura's shoulder to power her up. She

threw her hands up, and a wall of dirt rose out of the ground.

"Let's go!" she shouted.

Six of us ducked behind the earth shield she'd created—all three Fire Davina, our two partners, and Laura, who moved with us to keep us protected. We advanced forward, though the Infantry was only a hundred yards or so away from us now. Laura's shield hovered above the ground on her command.

"When you're ready, I'm going to create a break in the shield," Laura shouted. "Ready?"

Kellan glanced around the corner of the shield. "Go!"

Laura forced the dirt to part, and Celina, Caleb, and I all aimed our essence at the ground in front of the Infantry. Rain pounded down on them from above, but we created our fire just outside the range of Kaylee's storm.

The advancing men jumped back as fire ignited in a line in front of them. The flames were large at first, but quickly died down as they ate away at the manicured grass.

"Laura, we need more fuel!" I shouted.

She gritted her teeth and didn't tear her gaze from the dirt she was manipulating in the air in front of her. "I can't!"

Before anyone could give further instructions, the flames started growing higher. I glanced behind us to see Travis looking over one of the rubble piles and shooting me a thumbs-up. He was making the grass grow beneath our fire to fuel it.

Meanwhile, other Davina around the courtyard were flinging their elements at the men. Grass grew at their feet and tangled around their ankles, making them trip. Rocks flew through the air at speeds that could kill a person. Other Water Davina had joined in on Kaylee's storm, until the rain was pounding down so hard that we could hardly see the Infantry ourselves.

And still, gunfire rang through the air. I glanced around, and my stomach dropped when I saw how many people had fallen. There weren't many left standing.

"Where's everyone else!?" I yelled.

They should've been flooding out of their dorm rooms and trying to help, not hiding away like cowards.

Kellan ignored my question. "We've got this! As long as we—"

The sound of battle cries came from the other side of the crumbled building. The gunfire was deafening, and it hit me then that the Infantry had made it through the front gates of the academy. The huge group of men who'd come through the hole in the wall wasn't all of them—and they were still coming.

"Do we have enough elements to hold them off?" Shaylene asked. I was surprised at how level-headed she stayed.

Kellan shot a glance around the courtyard. "I don't know. There are too many people down."

"We have to get more Davina out here!" I shouted.

The earth began to shake more from the Davina controlling it. Ahead of us, a thick oak tree tipped over, making a loud smashing noise as it landed. Its roots tore up, leaving a huge hole in the ground.

Moments later, the horrible sound of cracking concrete met my ears. My eyes darted to the Winged Fountain not far from us, and my heart crumbled as the fountain split in two. The crack traveled all the way up from the base, until it reached the wings and one of them fell off and smashed into the pool below. Water sprayed everywhere, and it came pouring out of the broken base.

Someone somewhere began to control the excess water, and I watched wide-eyed as the water traveled in thick streams toward the new group of Infantry members. The water split in several directions and hit five of them in the face at once. Whoever was controlling it forced water up through their nostrils and down their throats. The five of them stopped in their tracks. Their mouths opened, like they were trying to scream, but nothing came out as water gurgled in their lungs.

I glanced back to my friends, taking my focus off my fire for a brief moment, to see that Everett was glaring at the incoming crowd with fury in his eyes. He twisted his hands, and the water followed his command. He ripped the water out of their mouths before they drowned, but it'd been enough to slow them down.

I was equally horrified as I was impressed.

"Watch out!" Kellan shouted.

From out of nowhere, a ball of glowing black Aedes essence whizzed toward us from the side. It was headed directly for Laura. She squealed and dropped her arms. Kellan jumped for her and tackled her to the ground. Laura narrowly missed being knocked out by the essence, but her shield had fallen. A cloud of dirt rose into the air, leaving us exposed. Bullets rained down around us, and the earth continued to shake.

Caleb let out a terrible cry and clutched his arm. Blood oozed between his fingers from where he'd been shot, but I barely had a chance to process the last second before Celina's hand was clutching my arm.

"This way!" she shouted, then dragged me and Shaylene behind the roots of the fallen tree.

"But Kellan!" I yelled.

I looked past the roots to see Kellan glancing around for me. He didn't see me, but it was obvious he didn't have time to waste. He threw his body in front of Laura and shielded her as they ran for cover behind the fountain. Caleb dove for cover beside them, and Laura threw up another earth shield.

Celina grabbed my arm before I could go run after them. She squeezed Shaylene's arm with her other hand and glanced between the two of us. "You run out there, you'll get yourself killed," she warned with an intense look in her eyes.

"But Caleb!" Shaylene protested.

"I know," Celina snapped. She took a breath to calm herself. "We'll find a way to get to him."

By now, the Infantry had swarmed all over campus. The three of us were crouched so low at the base of the rooted tree that no one noticed us. Yards in front of us, people ran across the courtyard, aiming weapons—both man-made and supernatural—at each other.

It was a freaking warzone! I didn't know how much longer we could hold out until the Alliance got here.

One of the Infantry spotted us. By the width of their shoulders and their hips, I'd guess it was a woman, but she was wearing a ski mask, so I couldn't see her face. She lifted her gun at the three of us, but we reacted quickly.

Three balls of essence whizzed through the air simultaneously—two white and one black. They slammed into her chest at the same time, and she went flying backward and landed hard on the ground. She'd been knocked out cold.

"We have to do something!" Shaylene cried, whirling back toward us.

I glanced between the two of them—a fellow Fire Davina, and an Aedes.

"All we've got is fire," I stated.

The girls shared a glance.

"Then if we're going to get back to our group, we know what we have to do," Celina said.

I nodded. Shaylene looked nervous, but after a moment of hesitation, she agreed. "Okay, I'll power you both up."

I already had enough power to sustain flames for days, but the extra boost would make me stronger.

Celina smirked. "Then let's light this place up, bitches."

Shaylene took a breath to steel her nerves, then held her hands out to both of us. We each took one, and we jumped out from behind the tree. Celina aimed fire on the left side of Shaylene, while I lit the ground to my right. Red-hot flames streamed out of my palms, and the grass in front of me went ablaze. Raging flames licked high above my head, until we couldn't even see the fight going on around us.

"That's really hot!" Shaylene cried.

"Keep going!" I insisted.

Celina and I created a sort of fire ring around us,

keeping back attackers and hiding ourselves from view. The flames followed us as we walked toward the fountain, creeping along the ground at our command.

When we reached the edge of the broken fountain, I breathed a sigh of relief and dropped my flames. I jumped over the edge of the fountain and into the dry base, where Kellan, Laura, and Caleb were hiding behind a mound of dirt Laura had created. She was hunched over Caleb and covered in blood.

"I can't…" she cried. "Kellan, I can't."

Caleb inhaled a sharp breath, but Kellan only reassured the two of them. "We'll find someone to help. You're going to make it, bro."

"We're here," I cried, coming to a halt as I landed on my knees. Blood dripped down Caleb's arm and pooled on the concrete below him. The bullet must've hit an artery for him to be losing blood so fast. His lips were void of color, and his eyes could barely focus on me.

"We have to stop the bleeding," Kellan demanded.

I didn't question it. I held my hand out to him, and he squeezed it tight. Essence poured through me, and I felt my healing magic well to the surface. I placed my hand on Caleb's wound, and warm, sticky blood coated my fingers.

But I didn't have a chance to heal him. A moment later, the sound of something metal clanging into the concrete fountain met my ears. I glanced to the side, and my stomach dropped out of my abdomen.

A grenade!

My friends and I leapt to our feet at the same time, all except Caleb, who could barely move from the blood loss.

"Run!" Shaylene shouted.

I barely had a moment to process what to do—because I knew Caleb wasn't going to make it to his feet in time. Shaylene shoved me out of the way as hard as she could, which sent me stumbling into Kellan. We both tripped over the side of the fountain. As we tumbled to the ground, the earth shot up around us, creating an instant hill. We couldn't control our momentum, and we went rolling down the hill and away from the fountain.

Boom!

The grenade went off before we'd stopped tumbling. Dirt went flying everywhere, and it was then that I realized the hill was another one of Laura's shields, but it was bigger than ever—at least ten feet tall, and it'd caused the sidewalk to heave up in all directions.

I lay on the ground beside Kellan, the two of us heaving and staring up at the shield Laura had made. It took a few moments for the shock to pass.

I looked upward to see Laura standing above us, her features strained and her hands held up to control the earth. She gritted her teeth a moment longer, before letting out a large sigh and dropping her hands to her side. The hill she'd created sagged a little, but it didn't go all the way back down to where it originally was.

Laura turned her head away, and Celina stepped forward. Gently, she pulled her into a hug. It was an unusual thing for Celina to do, but under the circumstances, it made sense.

Laura buried her face in Celina's shoulder. "I can't look," she whispered.

Kellen helped me to his feet. "Stay here."

The way he said it so firmly left my feet planted in the ground. It was like I couldn't move even if I wanted to.

Kellan stepped up the hill and peered over the side. I didn't need to see his face to notice his whole body sag at what he saw. Horrible images flickered through my imagination. Kellan turned to look at us, and all it took was a shake of his head for my heart to break into a million pieces.

"No!" I cried.

Kellan took several long strides over to me, until he wrapped me tight in his arms.

Beside me, Laura sobbed. "Oh, God. I didn't mean to leave them behind!"

"It's not your fault," Kellan told her while he rocked me back and forth.

I was shaking. Two of my best friends had just been killed. It wasn't real. It couldn't be. A wave of heavy emotions struck me all at once—denial, heartbreak, anger. I didn't know which one I felt more strongly at the moment, just that whatever it was made me ill beyond belief.

I lifted my head from Kellan's warm, comforting shoulder, to take in the chaos all around me. My friends had just been killed. Who knew how many other people had died tonight? And I literally didn't know how to stop it.

And then my eyes landed on *him*.

I didn't see his face, but I knew by the color of his hair and his build that it was him. Colt Walter slunk around the side of the Science Building.

"Kellan!" I cried, stiffening as my eyes locked on Colt in the distance. "It's him!"

Kellan glanced behind himself, but Colt was already gone. His eyes went wide. "You saw him? Colt?"

"Yes," I insisted. "We have to stop this."

I glanced to Celina and Laura. Laura's featured had quickly turned to pure fury. "You go," she said. "Celina and I have some Infantry ass to kick."

Kellan grabbed my hand, but I couldn't force my feet to move. I *wanted* to go after Colt. I wanted him to pay for everything he'd done. But a heavy weight like bricks settled in my guts—

Fear.

I was afraid of facing Colt.

But I couldn't allow myself to stall. I formed my hands into fists and let my anger push me forward.

Kellan and I raced across the courtyard in the direction I saw Colt go. We were more alert than ever, and we each shot essence at every Infantry member we saw, weeding them out one by one. As a man lifted his gun to us, I shot flames straight out of my palm and landed them on his knuckles. It was so hot that he dropped his gun and screamed in pain.

I didn't know how we did it, but somehow, Kellan and I made it across the courtyard unscathed. As we rounded the Science Building and away from the fight, we spotted two dark figures. The first was obviously Colt, and the second I didn't make out before he stepped into the building. All I could tell was that he was male and was taller than Colt.

Kellan and I stopped in our tracks and ducked behind

the bushes at the edge of the building. Colt glanced one way, then the other, but he didn't see us. He stepped into the building behind the other man.

"We have to get him to call off his men," I said to Kellan.

Kellan looked at me in a way he never had before. It was a warning—like I was about to make the biggest decision of my life. "Are you sure you want to do this? By any means necessary?"

I didn't know why, but in that moment, it was like I heard the words in my father's voice.

Are you sure you want to do this, Cora? What sort of legacy do you want to leave behind?

Legacy? I wondered. Right now, all I wanted was to prevent any more of my friends from being killed.

I wasn't my mother. Time and time again, she'd lectured me on sticking to my values, about doing the right thing. I knew that was how she won her battle twenty-five years ago, but it wasn't how I was going to win mine. Colt had too much blood on his hands—blood that I valued. And he was going to pay for that.

"Yes, Kellan," I said. "By any means necessary."

He squeezed my hand tightly. "Then stick close to me."

Kellan and I crept through the shadows, until we came to the door that Colt had entered. We quietly stepped into the building. A dark hall spanned in front of us, lit only by emergency lights every few yards. The hall was familiar, since this was where we had our Art of Healing labs every week. We could hear voices coming from down the hall, but it was hard to make them out.

"I think we can take them," I whispered to Kellan.

He nodded in agreement, then crept forward with me close at his heels.

"Why are you doing this!?" a woman cried.

My blood ran cold. It was Chancellor Harris!

Colt's evil laughter sounded down the hall. "To make an example out of the academy, of course."

Chancellor Harris scoffed. "I know why *you're* doing this," she sneered. "What I want to know is what's in it for *him*."

Kellan and I both exchanged a glance. Who was she talking about?

A familiar voice left me frozen on the spot. "It's just as he said, Casey," the man said smoothly. "I'm going to make an example out of you and your entire student body. No one will question keeping the supernaturals a secret again."

John Maddox!

I couldn't believe what I was hearing.

The Alliance was on Colt's side.

Something cold and hard pressed into my back between my shoulder blades. If I weren't already frozen in place, I'd have stopped dead in that moment. Instinctively, I knew it was a gun, and if I tried to fight back, I'd end up with a bullet straight through the heart. Kellan stiffened beside me, indicating he had the barrel of a gun pressed to his back as well. Slowly, we both lifted our hands in surrender.

"Move," a male voice demanded.

Kellan and I took a step forward. I tried to keep my knees from shaking, but I couldn't. I knew how to deal with injuries in a crisis. This was a whole other type of crisis. I didn't know whether I was supposed to fight back or stay calm.

The men behind us pushed us into the classroom where we studied Art of Healing. Chancellor Harris sat one of the chairs with her arms secured behind her back, while her husband lay unresponsive on the floor beside her. My guts twisted, and I hoped he'd only been knocked out. Three other men in suits stood in the shadows behind Maddox.

"We found these two lurking in the hall," one of the men said.

Maddox looked up from Chancellor Harris, the emergency lights casting deep shadows across his face. His features brightened when he saw the two of us enter the room. Colt wore a similar look of pleasure, but something about the way he was standing was strange. He stood to the side, like he was no longer the one in charge. It was actually a little terrifying.

The men holding guns to our backs stepped aside, and though the barrels were still trained on us, I felt like I could breathe now that it wasn't touching me. What I didn't expect was to see the men with the guns dressed in suits instead of ski masks. They were Alliance, not Infantry.

"Ah," Mister Maddox said brightly, opening his arms in a welcoming gesture. "Cora. Kellan. So nice of you to join us."

"Yeah, well, we couldn't miss the party," Kellan said coolly. "Mind telling us what's going on?"

Maddox eyed him up and down, as if deciding how much to tell him. Something in his features read amusement, like he wasn't at all offended by Kellan's demand for information.

"You realize you'll be dead before you have the chance to tell anyone," Maddox pointed out.

"Then we deserve to know what we're dying for," I stated simply, doing my best to keep my cool.

Maddox shrugged. "Very well. Secure them."

"What!?" I cried.

One of the men grabbed for my arms, while another shoved a gun in my face to make it clear not to struggle. I stilled and went with it, because I really didn't want to get shot in the face tonight.

The Alliance had come prepared. They didn't just find some old rope in the supply closet. They had handcuffs they secured behind mine and Kellan's backs before forcing us to sit in chairs they'd pulled up beside Chancellor Harris. I immediately glanced around, looking for a way out. We weren't exactly tied down to the chairs, but we'd never make it if we ran for the doors. My eyes landed upon a cart of dissection supplies a few feet behind me, not far from where Kane Harris lay on the floor. If I got my hands on a probe or even a sharp pair of tweezers, I might be able to pick my way out of the cuffs. But I couldn't get there from here.

"So, what is this?" Kellan demanded. "You've been working with the Infantry this whole time?"

Maddox began pacing in front of us. A hint of a smile touched his lips, like he was proud of how everything had played out and wanted to gloat about it. "No, Mister Greene. The Infantry was… convenient."

Kellan pressed his lips together. "Mighty convenient they attacked the same night you happened to be on campus."

Maddox chuckled in a way that made my skin crawl. "Oh, no, Mister Greene. *That* was no accident. You see, what you two did last semester has compromised all of us. You've made my job ten times harder trying to cover it up.

Your stunt has sparked quite an uproar within the Alliance —some saying we can't keep hiding forever, while others believe repercussions for exposure should be punished more severely."

"And what do you think?" I challenged before I could stop myself.

Kellan shot me this look, like he was warning me away from danger territory. I knew I might be heading there, but it was hard not to snap at this asshole with the massacre going on outside. I didn't have the luxury of keeping a level head at the moment.

Maddox stopped pacing and looked straight at me. "If it were up to me, Miss Marek, you'd have received the death penalty the second you exposed yourself."

"That's what this is about?" I asked. "You want to kill us?"

"Oh, don't flatter yourself," Maddox scoffed. "This isn't about some petty revenge. This is a sacrifice necessary to maintain the security and privacy of the supernatural community. Once the Alliance hears the death toll, they'll never consider letting our secret out again."

"There are people dying out there!" I exploded.

How could he not care? How could he justify the killing of his own people? People I loved had died tonight, and he was acting like that was some noble thing to be proud of.

"It's for the greater good!" Maddox roared, and I jumped in my seat. "The long-term benefits outweigh the short-term sacrifices."

"You call my friends' deaths *sacrifices*?" I snapped.

"Cora," Kellan hissed, warning me again that if I kept this up, I might get myself shot.

I pressed my lips firmly together.

Kellan looked to Maddox. "How'd the Infantry get involved?"

Maddox smiled, like he was proud of his mastermind plan. "The incident at the bank shook up a few Alliance supporters who believed it was time to expose ourselves, but it was clear they could not all be swayed. So I approached the Infantry myself and offered an exchange for their services."

"And what do they get out of this?" Kellan asked.

Colt got this crazy, blood-thirsty look in his eyes. "We get to kill your asses."

Maddox held up a commanding hand and spoke threateningly. "Mister Walter..."

Colt stepped back. It was amazing how much his demeanor changed when someone else was in charge. He was like a puppy bowing down to his master.

Maddox dropped his hand and crossed them both neatly in front of himself. "The deal was that I get Colt inside the school, and the Infantry goes hog-wild. They get the blood they've been looking for, and I get the assurance that the Alliance will continue to protect the supernatural race."

"How are you going to cover this up, though?" I demanded. "It's one thing to persuade the Alliance. It's another to persuade all the witnesses."

An evil smile spread across Maddox's face. "If the Alliance wants it bad enough, they'll find a way to cover it up. And believe me, after tonight, they won't let anything slip through the cracks ever again."

"It doesn't have to be this way," Chancellor Harris argued. "Sharing the truth may just save us. Just like it did when the Alliance formed!"

Colt stared down at her with an expression of utter disgust. "Don't you get it, lady? No one wants you here!"

Chancellor Harris's jaw tensed, and her nostrils flared. "Tell that to all the people we've healed."

Colt laughed. "I'll be sure to do that, if I ever meet one of them."

Beside me, I heard the sound of Kane Harris stirring. He was coming to, but I didn't think anyone noticed. His eyes fluttered open and met mine. My gaze flickered from his to the lab equipment beside him. He took one look at my handcuffs and knew what I was getting at. Slowly, so no one else would see him in the darkness, he reached for one of the probes, then tossed it into my hands. By some sort of miracle, I caught it, and my heart leapt in relief.

Chancellor Harris looked to Mister Maddox, but she spoke to Colt. "You realize you've sold your soul to a devil."

Colt crossed his arms and smirked. "Don't think I know what you are—all of you. After tonight, you'll all go back into hiding and never bother us again."

There was something darker in his eyes. He acted like he was fine with us going into hiding, but something told me he had plans to continue hunting us down once this was all over. Acting was the only way to keep himself on Maddox's good side.

"You realize that will never happen," Chancellor Harris said coolly. "We're everywhere."

Colt's eyebrow twitched, another sign that he had further plans he wasn't sharing. "That's not what your Alliance tells me."

Maddox smirked.

"He's lying," Chancellor Harris said simply. "Don't you see you're a pawn?"

Colt's jaw tensed. A second later, he swung his arm out, and his fist connected with Chancellor Harris's jaw. Her head snapped to the side, her blonde hair covering her face, but she didn't make a sound.

Maddox's hand shot out to grab Colt's wrist. "Don't you dare touch her. She's mine."

Chancellor Harris took a deep breath and sat upright in her seat again, like the punch had barely fazed her. She wore a look of stone cold resolve on her face.

Colt shoved Maddox off of him. "What do you care? You're going to kill her anyway."

"You think that gives *you* the right to lay your hands on her?" Maddox sneered. "You're not in charge anymore, Colt."

"I thought you said we were partners," Colt growled.

Maddox chuckled, but he spoke in a smooth, condescending manner. "Unfortunately, Casey was right. You got your Infantry here. You're no use to me anymore, and I can't have you trying to expose us again."

Maddox raised his hand, and fire formed within his palm.

"We had a deal!" Colt shouted, backing up and looking terrified.

Maddox stepped toward him, the flames in his hands licking higher. "I'm afraid our deal has changed."

Maddox drew back his hand, aiming the fire at Colt. My stomach dropped, but he never got the chance to land the blow. The earth began to quake around us. Lab equipment rattled on the shelves, and beakers vibrated off the countertops and smashed to the floor. The cart of lab equipment rolled across the room, and the Alliance members all shot their hands out to the sides to help maintain their balance. The earth quaked so hard that I could hardly focus on anything.

Maddox whirled toward Chancellor Harris. "You think that's going to stop me!?" he roared, training his fire on her as she controlled the earth beneath us with her essence.

Chancellor Harris chuckled. "No, sir. If anything is going to stop you, it's my husband."

The handcuffs I'd been picking gave way, and Kane and I jumped to our feet at the same time. Dark essence shot out of his hands. One ball of essence landed square in one of the Alliance member's chest, while the other whizzed by Maddox's head as he ducked. Both of my shots of essence struck two other Alliance members, knocking them out.

Everything happened so fast that I could hardly process it. Kellan jumped up, but his hands were secured behind his back, so he couldn't fight with essence. Instead, he swung his leg around and kicked the gun out of the nearest Alliance member's hands.

Chancellor Harris made a similar, but much more

impressive move. The rumors about her being highly trained in combat weren't exaggerations. When she stood, she kicked her chair so that it sailed through the air and landed square in the remaining Alliance member's face.

As Kane helped his wife undo her handcuffs, I whirled to help Kellan, and saw that the member he was fighting was twisting his hands to manipulate the air around him. Kellan gasped for air, and I knew the Davina was sucking the oxygen out of his lungs.

"Kellan, duck!" I shouted.

He followed my command, and my essence soared through the air and slammed into the Davina's chest, knocking him out.

Within moments, all of Maddox's backup were knocked out, leaving us to fight only Maddox and Colt. Chancellor Harris and her husband lunged for Maddox at the same time. She landed a kick to the chest, and I heard the sound of several ribs crack. Kane aimed his essence, but before he could throw it, Maddox reached into his coat and pulled out a Glock.

Before I knew what was happening, a *bang* went off, and Kane Harris stumbled backward, clutching his stomach. Kellan and I both jumped.

The earth began to rumble more fiercely under Chancellor Harris's rage. She jumped on Maddox so fast that she was nothing more than a blur. I ran over to Kane and applied pressure to the wound, my heart racing. He gasped for breath as blood poured out of his stomach and onto the tile floor.

"Kellan!" I cried. "We have to heal him!"

"My hands," he replied in a rush.

I jumped to my feet and grabbed the dissecting probe I'd dropped on the ground, then quickly picked Kellan's handcuffs. His hands broke free, and we both knelt beside Kane.

So much was happening at once that I could hardly process it. Chancellor Harris had knocked the gun out of Maddox's hands, and the two were fighting hand-to-hand now with moves I'd only seen in martial arts movies before. It was obvious they had both been trained in combat. Each time one of them tried to knock the other out with essence, they dodged it and landed another punch or blocked the other's blow.

Colt seemed to have frozen still. The doorway was blocked by the fight, so he couldn't leave the room even if he wanted to.

I barely had two seconds to take it all in, because Kane Harris was still bleeding out beneath me. Kellan grabbed my shoulder firmly, while I pressed both hands to the wound in Kane's abdomen.

My essence channel opened like a floodgate, sending magic flowing through me. I guided it down my hands, and they glowed as I worked my magic to stop the bleeding and heal as much of the wound as I could.

Kane gasped, but his breathing slowed as my essence filled him. "Good enough," he breathed. "Help my wife!"

Kane wasn't taking no for an answer. He shoved my hands away from his stomach, though he still wasn't completely healed. There was nothing I could do but continue to fight.

Kellan and I jumped to our feet again. Everything happened in slow motion, a split second passing in what felt like a minute.

Colt held a gun and aimed it at Chancellor Harris and Maddox. It was clear he was aiming at Maddox—that he was furious about the betrayal. Maddox landed a blow to Chancellor Harris's face, and she went stumbling to the side. He whirled around and noticed the barrel trained on him and acted instinctively. He lunged to the floor where his gun lay and grabbed for it.

"No!" I screamed, jumping for Maddox.

To be honest, I didn't care if Colt lived or died, not after all the terrible things he'd done to my friends. But we still needed him to call off the attack. John Maddox may have had the upper hand, but as far as the Infantry was concerned, they still took their orders from Colt.

"Cora!" Kellan cried. Before I could reach Maddox, Kellan's arm grabbed me around the waist, and I sling-shotted back into his chest.

Another *bang* sounded through the room, and I flinched. When my eyes opened, time seemed to be standing still. I didn't know who had made the shot—or if they'd hit anyone. Then blood began to soak into Colt's shirt, and time started forward again.

I lunged for Colt and caught him before he hit the ground. At the same time, Chancellor Harris had gone for Maddox, but he anticipated it. Maddox aimed essence at her, and she went down like a rock. Kellan and I were the only two left standing against Maddox.

"Kellan!" I cried. "We need Colt!"

But Kellan wasn't listening. Maddox pushed himself to his feet, but he moved like he was in pain. His hair was tousled at the top of his head, and blood dripped down the side of his cheek. His nice suit was all tattered.

"You two have been nothing but trouble for me!" Maddox growled. "The Alliance will move on from this easier with the two of you gone."

Maddox raised his gun and pointed it at me. Utter dread dropped through my stomach, but I barely had a split second to react before Kellan jumped in front of me.

"We're not going anywhere," he growled.

Then Kellan reached back to grab my hand, and essence unlike I'd ever felt it swept through me. This wasn't like the floodgates he'd opened before. This was like the whole damn ocean pouring through me all at once. As Kellan siphoned my essence through himself, it was like his desperation had opened my connection to the max, giving the two of us complete access to all the essence that flowed through the earth. My entire body glowed with essence so bright that it was all I saw. Even when I closed my eyes to block out the blinding light, it was still there, swirling around me and holding tight like a warm hug.

No, wait... That was Kellan. Kellan's strong arms wrapped around me, and his face buried into my hair.

"Hold on, Cora," he whispered.

And I did. I wrapped my arms around him and held on for dear life.

And then...

Boom!

The essence that'd been filling our bodies exploded in

one single blow. My eyes shot open, and all I saw was a huge ball of essence at least five feet wide spinning through the air at lightning speed, aimed straight toward the asshole with the gun on us.

He barely had time to react. All I saw were his eyes widening, then the essence blasted him back. Concrete went flying as the essence carried Maddox through the wall, blasting a hole straight through it and into the room across the hall. I'd never seen anything like it in my life.

I didn't need to see more to be sure—no one could survive that kind of blast. John Maddox was dead.

Complete silence fell over the room. I sank to my knees, my whole body quaking. Kellan wrapped me in his arms. I glanced below me to see that Colt had gone still. The life had left his eyes. And though I thought he deserved it, it was too much.

Tears poured over my lids and began streaming down my face. We'd lost our one chance at calling off the attack.

Maddox's men began to come to. But while I'd been crying, Kane had been limping his way around the room gathering all the guns. He stood in the middle of the room, black essence aimed at the Alliance members. As they all came to, it was the first thing they saw, and each of them stilled.

"I'm not going to kill you," Kane said through strained breath. "I want you to live with the regret of what you were a part of tonight. Now leave before I change my mind."

All five Alliance members glanced around. They saw the massive hole in the wall and must've thought better about sticking around, because they all scrambled to their feet and raced out of the room.

I sniffled into Kellan's arms. Moments of silence ticked by, but I still couldn't wrap my head around everything that happened tonight.

"How many do you think we lost?" I whispered into Kellan's shoulder.

Someone came up beside us, and I lifted my head to see it was Chancellor Harris. I hadn't even realized she'd woken yet. She looked terrible, but at least she was alive.

She held out her hand. "I don't hear any more gunshots. Should we go out and see?"

I wiped the tears from my cheeks and swallowed the lump in my throat. If there ever was a time to be strong during a crisis, now was it.

I took her hand, but I shook my head as I got to my feet. My gaze flickered to Kellan, who kept an arm wrapped around me.

"I don't want to just see," I said. "I want to do what I've been preparing my whole life for—I want to heal."

When we stepped out of the Science Building, it was like stepping through a portal into a post-apocalyptic world. But somehow, I found that comforting. There were no more sounds of gunshots, and the earth was still beneath our feet. The rubble remained, and fires burned through the lawn. Several people shouted each other's names, and others ran across the lawn as they searched for each other in the aftermath. But the fight was over. No more people would die.

Chancellor Harris supported her husband's weight. "John was blocking all communication with the Alliance tonight. I need to get a message to them. And Kane, we need to get you proper medical care."

He clutched his stomach. "Yeah," he said through gritted teeth. "I'm going to need surgery."

"Cora, Kellan," Chancellor Harris instructed, "find as many healers as you can, and start with the worst injuries. You know what to do."

Chancellor Harris left us alone. It was obvious that she didn't think us incompetent, as most adults did. Instead, she trusted us, much like the vibe I'd gotten from her at the beginning of the semester.

I stood in place a moment longer, dreading what we might find. Would more of my friends be gone?

Kellan took my hand. "Come on, Cora. We have to help."

Kellan's words struck me. *Help*. That was all I ever wanted to do—help people. I could grieve for the friends I'd lost later. Right now, I had to help those who still had a chance.

I squeezed his hand back. "Let's go."

Kellan and I walked forward, assessing the damage as we moved. There were so many bodies on the ground. I didn't even know where to start.

And then I spotted three familiar female figures bent over a male form. One of them was siphoning essence from the other two, while the Davina girls pressed their glowing hands on the guy to heal him. I was struck by the oddness of it, since I'd never seen a group of three heal together.

Kellan and I rushed over to Laura, Kaylee, and Celina. My stomach dropped when I saw that the guy they were healing was Travis. He had a huge gash across his chest, but it knitted back together under the girls' touch.

"Oh my God, you guys!" I cried. "You're alive!"

The three of them glanced up to us as we approached, but they didn't move as they continued to heal Travis.

Laura wiped the tears from her cheeks. "We're so glad to see you!"

Kellan furrowed his brow. "Wait. How are you two doing that?"

"Yeah," I agreed. "Kaylee, you haven't even studied healing."

"I don't know," she said. "Laura and I didn't even know we were compatible, but she touched me, and... it just came naturally."

"Same," Celina answered. "We didn't even mean to at first."

Travis stirred and inhaled a deep, refreshing breath. "I guess that makes me the lucky one tonight, huh?"

"Something's different," Laura pointed out. "I feel stronger."

"Me, too," Kaylee remarked.

My eyes widened, and Kellan and I exchanged a glance. We'd both experienced a huge surge of power back in the Science Building. Had the trauma we'd been through tonight built some kind of bond that strengthened our essence? I mean, Kaylee shouldn't have been able to heal without training. Yet here she was, healing with a total stranger.

I glanced around. There were so many bodies. Healing them could take hours—hours some of them might not have.

Kellan noticed the same thing I did. "You guys, how are we going to heal everyone?" he asked.

As I glanced down at Kaylee's glowing hands, something struck me.

"We need to get everyone we can together," I stated. "I have an idea."

Just as I said it, a group of guys came jogging over to us—Drew, Warner, Kumar, Miles, and Everett. Tucker and Jett were nowhere to be seen, and I worried we'd lost them, too. Warner was still favoring his broken arm, but it was clear he was going to make it.

"Everyone okay?" Drew asked breathlessly.

Laura swallowed, and her eyes darted in the direction of the fountain. She spoke in a small voice. "I think we're all that's left."

Travis sat up, his chest looking as good as new. "Cora says she has an idea."

Drew tilted his head to the side. "What kind of idea?"

I took a deep breath. "It's just a theory, but… do any of you feel a stronger connection with each other after tonight?"

Miles and Everett exchanged a glance, but it was Miles who spoke. "Everett and I just healed a girl's wing. We've never been able to heal together before."

The look in their eyes confirmed my suspicion. Tonight had brought us all together in ways we never thought possible. Which made our essence more compatible.

I kept one hand in Kellan's and reached out with the other for Drew. "Everyone join hands."

Drew glanced down at my outstretched hand and hesitated.

"It's okay," I told him. "I don't hold anything against you anymore. We stand together as one, remember?"

He nodded firmly.

"Which is why I think we need to do just that," I said to the group. "Everyone join hands."

No one questioned what I was doing. They all just followed along, trusting that whatever I had in mind was worth it. Laura helped Travis to his feet, and we all joined hands in a circle—even Warner, whose arm must've hurt like a bitch when Celina took his hand.

"Aedes, you know what to do," I said. "Davina… let your essence flow. Don't hold back."

"Got it," Travis said.

Celina glanced around the circle. "We stand together as one."

I'd never understood the truth of that motto as much as I did in that moment. As the Aedes around our circle began to siphon our essence, magic began to glow white in all of our hands. We began one unit, growing and shaping our essence until beautiful wisps of light came off our skin and swirled into a ball in the middle of our circle.

"We stand together as one," the group repeated.

Each time we said it, the wisps of essence grew and grew, until streams were pouring out from the middle of our circle, reaching out like blessed hands all across the courtyard. Our essence was so bright and spanned so wide that it lit up campus like the morning sun.

Beside me, Kellan squeezed his eyes shut tightly, until moments later, feathery black wings erupted from his back. When it happened, I felt my essence channel open to mega proportions, and I followed his lead. I flexed my shoulders, and white wings grew out of my back. All around the circle, everyone had noticed, and they followed suit until each of us were standing in our full supernatural form, an even mix of white and black wings.

The ball of light between us grew bigger and bigger, until it was blinding to look at. Warm, calm essence unlike anything I'd ever felt swirled out of me. As it intermingled with my friends' essence, I could feel the warmth of their magic brushing up against mine, then twisting together like an embrace. I felt our essence swirl across campus and touch the injured. Somehow, without seeing it with my own eyes, I could *feel* it.

My essence was healing.

And with each person we healed, I felt their essence give something in return, something more warm and comforting than I could've ever dreamed. It didn't matter who we healed—Aedes, Davina, or human. They all gave something in return, which fueled even more healing power for everyone else.

I didn't know how long we stood there. It could've been minutes, or it could've been hours. But as we healed those who'd fallen during the battle, one thing became very clear.

Too many humans had witnessed our healing tonight— had been *part* of it. We couldn't hide the truth any longer.

We all shared this world together.

It was time *everyone* stood together as one.

"Are you ready?" Kellan wrapped an arm around me and squeezed me close to him. It'd been days since the attack, but it felt like no time had passed at all.

I glanced to my friends and family surrounding me. Dad stood with his arm around Mom, who shot me an encouraging smile. She looked so vibrant and happy now that the restaurant had been rebuilt. Though she'd been severely burnt, there wasn't a scar left on her. It was great to see her back to her old self.

Kaylee stood beside me with a melancholy look on her face. Kumar had his arm wrapped around her shoulder. Next to them, Laura and Travis stood hand in hand. Beside them, Drew and Celina stood so close it should've bothered me, but it didn't. I actually thought those two would work well together.

The street was quiet as we stared up at the angel tree in front of the elementary school. It was summer now, so school wasn't in session. Some of the ornaments that had been placed there a few months ago had fallen off in the wind, but they'd been replaced. They sparkled in the sun just as beautifully as they had the first time I saw them, looking like diamonds swirling among the branches of the evergreen.

I took a deep breath and looked down to the ornament in my hand. Across the angel wings, Shaylene's name had been written in cursive. A lump rose to my throat as I thought about how we'd lost her—and so many others. She was so gentle and fun-loving. She would've been thrilled to see how we'd healed the entire courtyard with our essence.

Sometimes, I thought maybe she *did* see it—that her essence had combined with ours and she'd been with us to heal all those people.

She'd be proud of what happened afterward, how the Alliance had shown up to witness our healing, and how days later, after they had time to deliberate, they agreed that it was time to improve relations with humans, and not just those within government and special positions.

What came as the biggest shock was when Kellan's father, Ronan Greene, approached me himself and invited the two of us to serve on a new public relations council they were forming.

Kellan and I could hardly believe what we were being offered. It was what he always wanted—to serve on the Alliance and create policies that would make it easier for mixed families to assimilate into the supernatural world. This wasn't how he saw it happening, with us coming out in the open, but he would reach his goal nonetheless.

I took a deep breath and wiped a tear from my cheek. "Yeah," I said in an even voice. "I'm ready."

I stepped forward and hung Shaylene's ornament on the tree. Kellan placed the one with Caleb's name beside it, and the two clinked together. They started spinning until the strings were wound around one another. Each of my friends stepped forward and placed their own ornament on the tree, one for someone we'd lost.

My heart felt heavy, but as I stepped back and looked up at the sparkling tree, the weight began to lift.

It was far too quiet, but Celina took it upon herself to break the silence. She began to sing a melancholy tune, one that I knew her and Shaylene would've sounded perfect at in a duet. Normally, the sound of Celina's voice would've annoyed me, but it didn't. Right now, it was a comfort.

Laura reached her hand out to me, and I held on tight as we swayed back and forth to the sound of Celina's farewell song. Soon, everyone had joined hands and swayed to the same slow rhythm. Tears streaked my cheeks, and Laura sniffled from beside me. It was hard to say goodbye, but something about it was beautiful, too. I knew that wherever I went, the people I'd lost would be there with me, a part of my own essence. And their memory—their legacy—would live on.

Celina's voice faded, and everyone started pulling each other into hugs.

Mom and Dad wrapped me in their arms at the same time. Mom kissed the top of my head and said, "I'm so proud of you, Cora."

I drew away from her. "You are? But Mom, you never wanted me to fight like you did."

She swallowed, like she was on the verge of tears. "I didn't, but maybe you're not like me, Cora. There's a fire inside of you I never had."

I nudged her. "It comes from Dad."

My father chuckled, but his voice settled quickly. "Your mother's right, Cora. We're both very proud of you. You're going to do great things with the Alliance."

I smiled. "I hope so."

I glanced over to Kellan to see him and Celina exchanging a friendly hug. I knew he was deeply hurt by what she'd done to him, but he seemed like he was moving on from it now. Celina caught me eyeing her and walked over to me. My parents turned to Kellan, which left me and Celina alone.

"Hey, Cora," she said lightly. "I know we haven't always gotten along great, but after everything that happened... I just wanted to apologize."

Another few pounds seemed to lift off my shoulders.

"Look," she continued. "We're both really good at what we do, but I don't want to see you as competition. It got us nowhere during our final. I just don't want to be the bitch who ruins everything again."

I chuckled lightly. "Don't say that. You're not a... Well, you kind of were."

She crinkled her nose. "Yeah, I totally was."

"I want to put the past behind us, too," I said, but my eyes flickered toward Kellan. "I mean, as long as you don't consider us competition in *other* areas."

"Oh, God no," she laughed. "You don't still have eyes for Drew, do you?"

"He's all yours," I told her.

She smiled. "Good, because I was thinking of asking him out."

"Well, I guarantee he won't turn you down," I assured her.

"So, friends?" Celina asked.

I nodded. "Friends."

After Celina bounced away to go talk to Drew, Laura and Kaylee approached me again. The three of us shared a group hug. When we drew away from each other, Laura was the first to speak. "I'm so glad this is all over."

"Me, too," I said. "You went through so much."

Laura shrugged, but I could tell it bothered her. "Yeah, but it's finally over. I'll be in therapy for a while, but I know I'm going to get through this. I have you guys and Travis to help."

"And we will," I promised. "With anything you need."

She smiled. "Thanks."

"And I'll finally be at school with you guys," Kaylee said. "I'm sick of missing out."

Laura's eyebrows shot up. "Believe me, you should be glad you did."

Kaylee must've noticed the frown on Laura's face, because she quickly changed the subject. "Hey, what do you say we pamper ourselves later today? You deserve it."

"A mani-pedi?" Laura asked, her features brightening. "Are you a mind reader?"

The two of them walked off to talk about their plans for the day, and Kellan returned to my side.

"You were right," Kellan said as he draped his arm over my shoulder.

I looked up at him. "About what?"

"Hiding ourselves has only got us hurt," he clarified. "It's time to try something new and just… trust in the process."

"You're excited to be serving on the council, aren't you?" I asked.

"Do you even know me at all, Cora?" he teased, playing with a strand of my hair.

I pushed him lightly in the shoulder, but not enough to shove him away from me. "I'm glad you're looking forward to it."

He smiled lightly as he stared down at me with dreamy eyes. "I've been looking forward to it my whole life."

"I'll miss the academy," I said solemnly.

"Hey," Kellan said gently. "Joining the Alliance doesn't mean your studies are over."

"No," I agreed, "but I'm starting to think that maybe I'm not supposed to be a firefighter. Being on the Alliance *feels* right, but I'm going to have to change my whole course of study."

"As long as that's what you want," Kellan said. "You know you don't *have* to do this."

"I know," I said. "I want to."

"I'm glad to hear that. I get to do this with my girl at my side." He squeezed me harder, and my heart swooned.

"I'm glad, too," I whispered, before stepping up on my toes and planting a gentle kiss on his lips.

Kellan relaxed. "So, what do you want to do now? It sounds like Laura and Kaylee are leaving."

I glanced around, but no one was close enough to hear us. I lowered my voice to a whisper anyway. "To be honest, I'd rather be alone with you right now."

"Sure," Kellan said. "We could go grab a bite to eat or something—"

"No, Kellan," I chuckled. "I want to be *alone* with you."

I raised an eyebrow, and he quickly caught on. His mouth formed into a perfect O. His arms dropped from my shoulders, and he took my hands. "Well, that can be arranged."

"I should probably say goodbye to my parents first," I said.

Kellan's hungry eyes roamed over my body, and heat flared across the surface of my skin. "Hurry up, sweetheart."

My heart jumped when he called me that. He had no idea what sort of affect that had on me. He must've noticed my cheeks flush, because he asked, "You like that?"

I smirked. "A little."

"Hurry up, sweetheart," he teased.

I put my arms around his neck and pulled him closer, until his forehead was resting on mine. "The more you call me sweetheart, the more I want to stay right here in your arms."

He chuckled and pressed another kiss to my lips, then another, and another. A whirlwind of tingles spread throughout my abdomen and down between my thighs.

"Is that so, sweetheart?" Kellan teased.

"That's it," I said. "I'm never leaving."

Kellan's hands tangled in my hair, and he pulled me tight to him, until the side of my face was pressed tight to his chest. I could hear his heart beating, and it was the most wonderful sound in the world. Having him here in my arms eased the knot in my chest that'd been there for weeks.

"Then don't," Kellan whispered into my hair. "Don't ever leave."

"I won't," I promised.

And I meant it. Kellan and I had a future together. It wasn't the one I'd planned, but I guess sometimes life just surprised you. I never planned to fail my final exam our first semester. I never planned to expose ourselves as supernatural. I never planned to lose my friends like I had. Maybe the plan I had for myself wasn't the legacy I was meant to leave behind.

But one thing had never changed. All I ever wanted was to make a difference in this world.

Come hell or high water, I was making a damn good one.

THE END

This concludes Cora and Kellan's story, but the Davina have more adventures! Don't miss Cora's parents in the Divine Fate Trilogy.

ABOUT THE AUTHOR

Alicia Rades is a USA Today bestselling author of young adult and new adult paranormal fiction. When she's not dreaming up magical stories, she's either binge-watching paranormal TV shows, meditating, or spending time with her family. She has an unhealthy obsession with psychic characters and writes with a deck of tarot cards next to her computer.

www.ingramcontent.com/pod-product-compliance
Lightning Source LLC
Chambersburg PA
CBHW031558310726
48974CB00003B/726